Nayantara Sahgal is the author of
and non-fiction, the first of which .... and *Chocolate
Cake*, an autobiography, was published in 1954. Her works
include classic novels such as *Rich Like Us*, *Plans for
Departure* and *Lesser Breeds*. She has received the Sahitya
Akademi Award, the Sinclair Prize and the Commonwealth
Writers' Prize. Her novel, *When the Moon Shines by Day*,
was longlisted for the 2018 JCB Prize. She returned her
Akademi Award in 2015 in protest against the murder by
vigilantes of three writers, and the Akademi's silence at the
time. She has been a Vice President of the PUCL (People's
Union for Civil Liberties) and is engaged in an ongoing
protest against the assaults on the freedom of expression
and democratic rights.

THE FATE OF BUTTERFLIES

Nayantara Sahgal

SPEAKING
TIGER

SPEAKING TIGER PUBLISHING PVT. LTD
4381/4, Ansari Road, Daryaganj
New Delhi 110002

First published in hardback by Speaking Tiger 2019

ISBN: 978-93-88874-05-2
eISBN: 978-93-88326-88-9

10 9 8 7 6 5 4 3 2 1

Typeset in Arno Pro by SŪRYA, New Delhi

There may be trouble ahead,
But while there's moonlight and music
and love and romance,
Let's face the music and dance.
Before the fiddlers have fled,
Before they ask us to pay the bill, and while we still have
that chance,
Let's face the music and dance.

—From the film, *Follow the Fleet*, 1936

He sat at a table near the window looking down on the blue and purple cluster of potted hydrangeas at the entrance, and beyond the pavement puddles to the rain-drenched monsoon light of the August morning. A steam bath outdoors but air-conditioned to pleasant coolness in the restaurant, not to an Arctic freeze. He was comfortable in cotton. Bamboo-framed watercolours of flowers and foliage by French artists brought a European springtime to the room. The wall-hanging opposite had a Tree of Life in blossom, delicately hand-painted in rose, cream and crimson dyes. Its original had been designed, he had been told by the owners, for the flower-loving Mughal emperor, Shah Jahan.

Bonjour was a breakfast retreat he had discovered on his previous visit to Delhi six months ago, and breakfast was being served. Not his hotel buffet with something for all comers from smoked salmon to items labelled idlis and parathas, here it was served on order, à la carte, granting respectful attention to the day's first meal in recognition of a day that for many of its patrons would demand every ounce of concentration, and if negotiating minds were not already made up, skilled persuasion. Tables were spaced to allow conversation that neither intruded nor was overheard by others. He felt he was back in a civilized era before noise became endemic.

Coffee was a treat. It came, as before, in the common clay 'kulhar' in which, he had been told, tea had always been served by tea vendors at railway stations and roadside stalls but had now been discarded in favour of dingy cups and mugs. He dissolved a teaspoon of brown sugar crystals in his coffee, stirred it, and took a meditative sip. It had never had this earthy richness or aroma drunk out of china. Francois and Prahlad, the couple who owned Bonjour, clearly had a genius for combining the best of both their worlds, the one French, the other Indian. Prahlad saw him and smiled. He walked over, stepping with the nimble grace of the dancer he had been, rested a hand on Sergei's shoulder by way of welcome and went on his way, leaving Sergei to order and eat in peace. He ordered Eggs Benedict. The menu informed him that hollandaise sauce on poached eggs had been thought up in the kitchen of New York's Delmonico restaurant, and was not as he had fancifully supposed, a creation of the Benedictine order of monks whose spiritual ardour had not interfered with their taste buds if the liqueur named after them was any indication.

Two breakfasters at a table near him were foreigners like himself, but young black-haired men. They had their briefcases with them, presumably going straight on to their business appointments, and a file open between them, conferring while they ate. They looked fresh out of courses in markets and management and as focused as any samurai on their targets—unlike himself who at their age had been reluctantly weaned from the classics and a desire to write, to be trained for the future his father had so resolutely built. But that apart, the young men belonged, like him, to the tribe of frequent travellers for whom travel meant flying visits and distance had no literal meaning, with any country an hour or a night's flight away. A far cry from the plodding journeys of centuries past, on foot or mule or camel, on wheels or sea-craft at the whim of sea winds, by traders risking the perils of travel to peddle their wares. An unlikely beginning it had been to the saga of seizure, occupation and empire that trade became. The old *Punch* cartoon showing Cecil Rhodes triumphantly astride Africa from Cairo to the Cape with a rifle slung over his shoulder, told the story. A fascinating subject, the story of trade.

His own business had been completed yesterday. The discussion had gone over the ground covered six months ago with some major additions, and had confirmed the decisions taken. The same senior civil servant, worthy successor to the steel frame that had administered British India, had chaired it with professional ability. A disappearing breed, he had heard it said. There had been two other men present, one of them apparently an official whose specialized knowledge was needed for final purchase orders. The other man had been introduced, but vaguely. Sergei had not caught his designation but his presence seemed to be more than that of a trustworthy aide required to sit in and report. The hint of deference towards him implied something more. Either way, an extra presence was usually the sign of a new political dispensation.

The meeting had taken place in the same room as last time but Sergei had noticed changes. A decorative display of swords and daggers with handles of intricate elaborate craftsmanship and shining sharp-edged blades adorned one wall, and were obviously collectors' items chosen by weapons enthusiasts. And entirely different portraits commanded the wall space above the sofas. New founding fathers? He was reminded of his father's bleak joke from Soviet times, with one nervous apparatchik asking another, 'Let me know Who's still Who.' It also took his mind back to a side street in a Lusaka backwater where a poster painter kept posters of rival politicians stacked for sale because 'You never know.' Sergei had been amused and impressed by this gem of street wisdom and the man's grasp of the way things were. Quick change was the name of the game when power changed hands overnight as in coups and sudden takeovers, and during post-imperial slugfests for control in shaky national situations, but a clean sweep of founding fathers was the last thing he would have expected in the democracy that was the republic of India.

For Sergei it had become a matter of observation, not opinion, a cardinal rule of commerce being its distance from politics, but political riddles of this sort were intriguing.

'We only make use of the opportunities politics provides,' his father had made abundantly clear, and there had been plenty of those during the Cold War, like the upheaval in Indonesia that overthrew Sukarno in 1967.

'The new regime under Suharto swung into action right away disposing of Communists,' Dimitri had told him, and lest his son and future heir have misgivings about the manner of it and demand to know why—the kind of question Dimitri had asked himself in a time gone by and knew it had no answer—he had tutored Sergei in the workings of power: 'There will always be those who call the shots and those who bear the brunt—not our concern.' He had added, with the detachment that accounted for his success in the manufacture and sale of armaments, that all sides had profited from the Communist bloodbath. It had earned Suharto America's pleasure and brought billions of dollars into Indonesia's petroleum industry. President Ford and his secretary of state, Henry Kissinger, had enjoyed a cordial dinner with Suharto and given him carte blanche to invade and occupy East Timor. This he did the day after the dinner party, first thing in the morning. Dimitri recalled the massive military operation that had needed the most advanced weaponry from him and other suppliers.

Sergei knew his father for the complex character he was, too discerning a mind to be boxed into the crude either/or of the Cold War. He knew Dimitri had no love for either side. He had been a Communist and true believer until Stalin's show trials and purges forced him to flee with his knowhow and his secrets into exile, escaping the single blinding light, the inquisitor's dark shape at the desk, and certain death. His commitment to the cause he had served had died instead. If the grandeur of Lenin's vision had been so treacherously and blithely sabotaged, if Trotsky, its last surviving hope, was later hunted and murdered in far-off Mexico, then what chance had any dream, or the dreamer, of survival? Robbed of the faith he had lived by and with no place on earth he could think of as home, he had built his second life on his past experience with support from the French who had given him asylum.

'Alfred Nobel was very upset when a French newspaper called him "a merchant of death" for having invented dynamite,' he told his son, 'The newspaper described him as a man who had "found ways to kill more people faster than ever before," and so Nobel got himself remembered for prizes instead of armaments, including a peace prize. But many another roaring trade has as much and more to answer for, Sergei. Cotton was grown by slaves. Slaves planted cane and made sugar out of it. Slaves extracted rubber and got their hands and feet chopped off if they didn't produce the right amount, and diamond miners were stripped to check them for hidden diamonds and got their hands cut off if they were caught stealing. You could say trade of all kinds has blood on its hands. And then there are children working on plantations—it's cheaper.

'As for the sanctity of human life, Sergei, who remembers Bikini was where the H-bomb, which was equal to twenty-nine thousand A-bombs, was exploded, now that it's a wisp of sexy swimwear? Or that Lumumba was killed for winning an election that Belgium wanted him to lose, and wasn't the name of a Congolese cocktail? But shake up milk and cocoa, add cognac and pour it over ice cubes— in the world we live in, that's a Lumumba.'

Sergei, Paris-born and British-bred, had inherited a going concern complete with his father's handed-down access to those who mattered. Otherwise, except for his fluent Russian, inheritance was missing. Not so much as a stray snapshot had survived the flight from the homeland. Nothing either to inspire or offend. It was a strange situation he had come to accept. No remembered sight, smell or taste had been bequeathed to him in a deliberate burial of memory. His mother had talked yearningly of the life they had left behind but she had died in a car collision, though in reality of exile, when he was a child. His father, abruptly widowed, had no reason left to look back, memories being of no use to a survivor who had no one to share them with. Dimitri lived intensely in the present he had carved out for survival. Sergei wondered what he would have made of the swords and daggers, and the new founding fathers. He was finishing his breakfast when Prahlad joined him.

'How long are you staying this time, Sergei?'

Longer, he said, to give himself time to relax and look around. Prahlad patted his hand approvingly and said he hoped this didn't mean only monuments and museums.

'Don't forget we're here, too, Sergei! You must meet a dear friend of ours. And I will be dancing for a special occasion. You must come.'

Back at the hotel Sergei found an invitation from

The Fate of Butterflies

the American ambassador to dine at the embassy the following evening.

∽

Books had their unexpected ways of getting started. This one had begun when Prabhakar turned his car into the driveway, not noticing the new name on the gate.

The young woman looked up as the car drove in. Cars were not supposed to come in. The gate was kept closed so that no child could run out on the road. But there it was in the porch with someone getting out of it and surveying the scene.

Prabhakar saw the young woman getting up from where she sat on a durrie on the grass among small and very small children. Two or three of the smallest jumped up too. It was a pretty picture, the young woman surrounded by children, and it had a familiar ageless charm. It got him idly wondering why some images stick and others fade. What was it that made some images and ideas live on and become the bedrock of our beliefs and values? He walked up to her.

17

'Can you tell me where I can find him?' he asked, giving his friend's name after greeting her.

He had been away for some time and he didn't know the house had changed hands, or that it had become a school, he said. She disentangled a child's grip on her sari and shook her head.

'The house is not a school. It belongs to a friend who lets us use the garden for our nursery school. It's for two-to-six-year-olds. There are the verandahs and that big sheltered terrace for when it rains,' she told him, 'We run it ourselves. Parents take turns. The three of us are parents.'

She waved a hand behind her. Two women her sort of age were supervising the activities of boys and girls with a notable lack of supervision. One or two were getting no help clumsily pushing coloured wooden beads onto a cord. Older ones were plastering sheets of paper with randomly chosen colours from their paintboxes and some were chalking unrecognizable squiggles all over a blackboard. A few were sitting at a long low stone table drinking juice. He noticed the juice was being drunk out of glasses, not disposable paper cups.

The table was covered with a starched white cloth and laid, to his astonishment, with peony-patterned porcelain china.

'We give them lunch before they go home,' the young woman explained, and seeing him staring at the table, 'This is how we get them used to beautiful things and to handling them with care. You'd be surprised how careful children can be. The glasses and china belong to our friend who owns the house.'

A joyful shriek from the infant at her side made her bend down swiftly to prise open his fist. The crushed butterfly fluttered faintly and lay still. Another feeble flutter of its papery purple wings, and then to her evident relief, it flitted upward and away.

She looked up at Prabhakar in indignant appeal. 'Can you believe some schools teach children to collect butterflies and kill them? Did you know butterflies get thirsty and like to settle on wet leaves for drops of water?'

He didn't know and he was ready to leave but she was still talking.

'It's easy then to catch them in nets and kill them.

19

NAYANTARA SAHGAL

There's a horribly cruel technique to it. First you have to squeeze the poor thing through its middle to cripple it and then put it in a jar with some acid stuff for a couple of hours. That's how long it takes to be sure it's dead. After that you take it out and stick a pin through its middle and frame it in the same frame with all the other butterflies you've killed. Is that the way to teach children about nature?'

'I mustn't keep you from your work...'

That's quite all right and would he like to know more about the school, she asked? Prabhakar was about to decline, tactfully, so as not to hurt her feelings. He was impatient to be on his way, and would have taken his leave if the ghost of an idea had not crossed his mind. He stayed.

'We feel parents should be connected with their children's education right from the start,' she was explaining in her earnest fashion, 'That's why we don't have teachers teaching them at this early age. We don't believe in telling them what to do and making them memorize things. We want them to use their own minds and to experiment. Art and handicrafting are good ways to begin to do that, don't you think? Besides,' she continued anxiously, 'we want them to respect living things and be sensitive to their surroundings. We want them to grow up to be caring and kind and...,' she thought hard for the right word, and settled for 'well, good, kind people.'

And the opposite of all that had got the book started and finished in record time.

Dinner at the American embassy was informal. Sergei knew no one except his hosts, the Judsons. The other five guests were Indian and seemed to be on first name terms with each other. One husband was a known name in the media, another in ruby and sapphire mining. Over bourbon and bonhomie the talk was animated and cheerfully political, everyone agreeing that things had never been better.

Jake Judson explained the good cheer to Sergei. The new regime had brought in major changes. Opened up. Taken sides with the right people. Got off the fence at long last.

'They've got real,' Jake summed it up with vigour, 'You can see they mean business. You can see the adrenalin flowing. The change has been a long time coming. How did your meeting go?'

It had gone excellently, Sergei told him. But how about these major changes that everyone was agreeing about? 'Did you pick your guests so there'd be no arguments to spoil dinner?'

Jake laughed heartily, 'Nothing like that. Ask Linda. She picked the guests. These are the people who enjoy her down-home Southern cooking. Lindy thinks the world needs educating about the South. She's from an old Virginia family. Confederate folks. Incidentally, you don't have to drink Jack Daniels. You can have Scotch if you prefer. Lindy won't hold it against you.'

Sergei said the bourbon was welcome, and held up his glass to salute Lindy across the room. She blew him a kiss in return.

'Tell me about the major changes, Jake.'

Jake said he would get Kritik—'He's the bright guy who edits an influential weekly'—to put Sergei in the picture over dinner, but his own reading was that the warrior caste had taken over, they being number two in the caste hierarchy. 'You could give them the credit for the turnaround in policy and the business-like way they are getting things done. It takes a military mind to get down to brass tacks.'

At dinner pulled pork took the place of major changes. 'Why is it called pulled pork, Lindy?' from one of the wives. 'Because it has to be cooked real slow in a heavy pot for hours until it gets so tender and juicy, you can pull it apart. This is a Louisiana recipe.' It was agreed that no meat had ever tasted as succulent. Unheard of accompaniments called sweet potato casserole, Southern creamed peas and buttermilk biscuits upheld the pork's high standard and Dixie pie was greeted with acclaim. A mellow company moved to the drawing room for coffee and brandy. No one was in a hurry to leave. Major changes were forgotten.

'How's the family?' Lindy asked Sergei.

His son was working in the New York office, he told her, and his daughter had just had a baby. Susan was revelling in grandmotherhood. He and

Susan were getting on so much better since they had separated.

'That's so true, isn't it?' remarked Lindy of separations and divorces, and then of marriage, 'The first time you marry is a trial run, like the first waffle. You have to discard it.'

Back at his hotel Sergei rang his daughter. It was the right time for London. 'How are you, darling? Are you all right? How's the baby?'

'We're both fine, Daddy, don't worry, and she's the sweetest. You'll love her. I'm breastfeeding her. On demand, not by the clock, so I'm up at all hours but it's good for both of us.'

Sergei worried about Irina—named after his mother—about her health, her happiness and above all, her politics. Of his two children she was the one he worried about. Slight, soft-voiced and slenderly built, Irina looked appealingly feminine and vulnerable. The contrast could not have been greater with the views she held dear, and activities of the kind that were much better left alone. He was hoping motherhood would change all that.

'Are you enjoying your time off, Daddy? What have you been doing?'

'I've been eating Louisiana cooking. Pulled pork and Dixie pie.'

'But I thought you were in India.'

'I am. This was at the American embassy.'

'Oh no!' in dire dismay, 'How could you? After they invaded Iraq for oil they had no right to, and Vietnam before that and the atom bomb before that. And the gun lobby in full swing over there.'

'But it was a good dinner.'

She laughed. She hadn't mentioned his own arms-dealing and never did. Sergei knew this was not out of any concern for his feelings but because of her conviction that 'People have to realize for themselves. It's no good shoving ideas down their throats.'

'Anyway, Daddy,' she said, 'think of a name for the baby. A beautiful name.'

He promised he would think of one soon.

During a sabbatical from teaching, Prabhakar had taken a break from political science and written a lighthearted book about the why and how of societal changes with a chapter on changing fashions in clothes. The idea had caught his fancy on a flight from Delhi to Mumbai, flipping through a lavishly illustrated fashion magazine that had been left on the seat beside him and reading that women's wear had radically changed during the French Revolution. It had been liberated from imprisoning corsets and innumerable voluminous petticoats. Change is what fashion does, but what had brought about an inside-out makeover as dramatic as this? Exploring the period he came to the conclusion that the fashion revolution had nothing to do with the great Revolution's liberty, equality or democracy. It had happened because American cotton cloth and English (though really Indian) cloth was flooding the French market. Cotton in all its weaves and variations, from fine to finer to weightless and transparent, was all the rage in France.

Prabhakar, freed from the classroom, had let his imagination take over. It must have been the first time since Grecian antiquity that a garment had been allowed to flow down a woman's body with no hooks or wires or stiffening, no bulk or coarse fabric to impede its flow. Gauzy muslins revealed glimpses of the long-barricaded, suffocated feminine form in all its allure and desirability as nature had designed it. Hair got liberated too. No more rigid styling, it was no longer rolled, crimped, powdered or wigged, just gathered into the most casual of buns that a touch would unloosen to spill out.

Prabhakar pictured Josephine and her women friends clad in the blissful heady freedom of cotton in her salon at Malmaison among admirers and would-be lovers. With intimacy within hand's easy reach, seduction had never been so effortless, and what could be more natural now that Josephine's most infatuated lover—her husband—was away conquering Europe. Was it her infidelity that had led to her dismissal from Napoleon's bed and would she have remained his adored mistress even after he divorced her to marry royalty but for the cotton that had flooded Europe?

And so to the next question. Would the French

market have been flooded with foreign cotton and French women so enticingly robed but for slave labour in America and England's rapacious plunder of India? The personal and the political thus, as always, inextricably entwined. French fashion's romance with cotton had lasted until Napoleon banned its import to encourage France's own silk manufacture, but Prabhakar had not been able to resist adding the teaser: And who knows why else Napoleon banned cotton, making way again for corsets and petticoats and iron control of women's bodies.

Reviewers had shrugged off Prabhakar's humorous take on societal change. Entertaining but. A bit beyond poetic licence, or, if there was such a thing, academic licence. And to what purpose? What was the point of taking liberties with history?

'I'm not the first to do it,' said Prabhakar, but his interviewer had not heard of the hilarious English classic, *1066 and All That*.

Prabhakar took time to explain. It was his conviction that the personal and the political were inseparable. Private matters, even the most intimate, could make a decisive difference to the course of history. Think about it, Napoleon might have won the Battle of Waterloo and Europe's future would have gone on being Napoleonic for who knows how long if it hadn't been for his haemorrhoids. He had a terrible attack of haemorrhoids on the morning of the battle and had not been able to get on horseback to inspect the battleground, so he couldn't plan, as he always did, the course of battle. It was a fatal omission. The interviewer said it was a good story but history was not about what might-have-been. Prabhakar persisted. Political events—whether they made history or not—had to be seen in terms of human beings, the men and women who took part in them. You had to make room for personality and even for bowels—like Martin Luther's chronic constipation. The sixteenth-century German professor of theology, who later became a priest and monk, had spent hours sitting on his toilet seat. That's where visitors met him. It was where ideas came to him. Sitting on that stone potty he wrote his famous ninety-five heresies challenging the Catholic church. The fact is the Protestant Reformation was born out of Luther's chronic constipation.

The expression on the interviewer's face implied: What next in outlandish examples? But Prabhakar carried on, saying what's more, you could never leave out the unexpectedness of the human spirit.

'Such as?'

Such as... but it was a poem his friend Rahman who taught literature had read to him that came to mind. Trapped in the hell of trench warfare the English poet had not written, as you might expect, about his dread of his head being blown off any minute, but of laughter, peace and gentleness— those were the words in the poem—and of himself as 'a body of England's, breathing English air, Washed by the rivers, blessed by suns of home...'

Prabhakar was a popular (not yet full) professor, known for taking his students on journeys beyond the text, and his book had delighted those who were familiar with his mix of politics with its human side. There had been enjoyable exchanges about it in and outside class.

Back to teaching, he had not given the subject

of societal change another thought until the day of the nursery school in the garden. It had got him wondering what made an idea like kindness or compassion (even for a butterfly) become a mark of civilized behaviour. How had it happened that in times indifferent to suffering there had appeared men who were obsessed with the suffering of others? A prince had renounced princedom in his lifelong search of a cure for it. A prisoner in the agony of crucifixion had prayed for his torturers: 'Father forgive them.' An emperor wept after victory in war, appalled by the carnage, and vowed never to make war again. Men who were out of the ordinary. In a world without pity, in the savagery of their times, they had envisaged another world and made a religion of compassion.

He had intended to write a new book about the lasting impact of these men, but another narrative had written itself, the truth being that their impact had not been lasting.

On the other hand, the everlasting indifference to suffering was vividly documented and in great detail. He did not need invention or imagination to describe it, as he had in his word-play about the pleasures of promiscuity in muslin. What baffled was the matter-of-factness of cruelty. A man had thought nothing of hammering nails through the living flesh of another man's hand. A man had operated the rack that stretched another man's joints beyond human endurance a fraction at a time. Practice had perfected and refined techniques. The terror of men and women delivered alive to ravenous beasts in the Roman arena had been popular entertainment. It was not hard to picture the Romans who thronged the terraces getting an afternoon's thrill from the spectacle of human flesh in animal jaws. All this had happened and gone on happening in its infinite imaginative variety.

Specifically, his narrative had taken the turn it did because driving home from the nursery school that day, he had had to lurch sideways and brake violently to avoid running over a body that had suffered the fate of butterflies, but bloodily axed, not pinned, through its middle. It lay spreadeagled on the road, naked but for the skullcap on its head, with the axe left propped against its side, two signatures announcing: This is why and this is how. Was this a sign of things to come for those whose faith was Islam? Prabhakar had fallen forward on the steering wheel and lost track of time. When he straightened up, drizzle was spattering the windscreen, blurring vision. He got the wipers going and started the car. By the time he reached a crossing, rain was slamming the roof of his car. He had to shout through the window to the traffic policeman who said, yes, yes, we know, we will be removing it, and waved him on.

His book was out. Classes had resumed after a short break. He had driven to the university, past the tank at the entrance, its turret pointed at entrants. It had become a fixture he hardly noticed any more. His classroom was half empty, holiday lag quite likely. He had started to speak when a girl in T-shirt and jeans stood up in the back row and screamed, 'How could you? How could you write a book like that?' and was gone before he could say he would talk to her later.

'A brilliant book,' the vice chancellor said, stopping him in the corridor after class, 'Extremely well put, the point you make. I congratulate you.'

Prabhakar acknowledged the compliment warily. The new—now some months old—vice chancellor was the one who had requested the tank, to instil spine into the students. The VC turned around at the end of the corridor and called, 'Can you look in tomorrow morning for a few minutes? My office, at ten?'

Prabhakar raised a hand in assent.

Someone was with the VC in his office next morning. He had come with a letter for Prabhakar and been told to bring back a verbal reply. To save time, the VC explained. Prabhakar opened the letter and read the few lines from, good God surely not, the eminence whom he and one or two of his colleagues called the Master Mind, the man who was head of the regime's policy-making cell, inviting him to his house tomorrow at four: '...people you will be interested in meeting in view of your

34

book…' Ten seconds, twelve, were long enough to read the brief note. He sat saying nothing for much longer. The VC and the official messenger were in amiable chit-chat. Prabhakar racked his brain for a reason to refuse. The VC turned to him and smiled understandingly—a letter from on high, after all, quite natural to be a little awed—and then said, 'Of course you must be a relation of…'

'No, no, I'm not,' Prabhakar hastened to reply, wondering if that could be the reason for the letter? Whatever the reason he could see no way out. He would have to go and get it over with. He told the messenger he would be there.

Four o'clock tomorrow would come when it did, it was seven o'clock this evening that concerned him, drinks at his apartment to which she had said she would try and come. He was sure she meant what she said and was not putting him off in a polite way. It could be the nature of her work that made her uncertain and if so, the thought of it drove him to an anxiety close to desperation. The art of loving demanded that the loved one be shielded from all danger, a rule to be religiously adhered to, but it was one he was helpless to do anything about.

Prabhakar got into his car, drove out past the tank and turned right, heading for the shopping mall that had everything. The friends he had invited would be coming in any case even if she didn't, so drink and snacks had to be bought and ordinarily nuts and Haldiram's crunchies would have been enough for a usual casual get-together, but if she came… He knew nothing about her likes and dislikes. He only knew what he had read about her at her trial and the brutally frank and hair-raising account she had given of all that had happened. He had never expected to meet her. And then he had met her, last week, at Francois's place. And his future had become unthinkable, inconceivable without her. The time came to say goodbye all round, walk to the door and out into the corridor where his hand on the door should have clicked it shut behind him. But he had gone in again like a man possessed to ask her if by any chance she might perhaps be free on Wednesday evening, around seven o'clock, and just in case, had jotted down his address on the paper napkin beside her. He had hardly expected her to say yes to a stranger, was overcome by her maybe, and this was how she might be coming, or not coming, this evening at seven.

He made his way to the cheeses. At Francois's he remembered seeing her break off a bit of biscuit, push it into a ripe soft cheese and scoop up the melted part in the middle. Its name was unknown to him. He described what he needed to the salesman behind the counter who asked, 'Do you want Swiss or French?' Prabhakar had no idea but at Francois's it might have been French. He walked past the Parma ham, lingered at rows of high-priced foreign tins and bottles and picked up Spanish olives, an Italian artichoke paste and a jar of anchovy-garlic spread. From the wine section, a French wine he recognized. He went back to the Parma ham. Watched it being sliced razor-fine and layered on waxed paper which was then neatly folded and packed for him to take home. He was not spending sensibly and was well aware that sense had little to do with the state of being known as enchanted.

In the car his phone pinged. A high whining voice thanked him sing-songly for 'shopping with us and we hope you will visit our cheese counter again and our'—he switched it off.

'What's this, a celebration?' exclaimed Rahman. Salma, his wife, surveyed the spread and said, 'Of course, silly, the new book!' She traced an exaggerated adab to Prabhakar before throwing her loving arms around him.

There was no way to explain it was not about the book. The others were coming in. The room was filling with affection and exuberance and suddenly with celebration. At its high point Lopez tapped a glass for attention and raised his own to hail the book by 'the brainiest, luckiest, and goddammit it's not fair, he's even the best-looking bastard of us all!' Prabhakar responded to the high spirits around him with equal abandon, agreeing with Lopez. Privately his gratitude for fortune's favours knew no bounds. He had friends he could not imagine being without, work of his choice and a satisfying life. It was too much to expect another favour yet every nerve in his body ached for the doorbell to ring. Glances at his watch told him what he already knew, that time was passing. At half past eight he gave up hope. Hours later he woke abruptly and lay awake endowing the tank and the sing-song litany on the phone with sinister possibilities. He had not known that fear was the other side of love. His last waking thought was of her, held safe in his sheltering arms.

The house was in a crescent of private houses. Prabhakar was warmly greeted.

'I thought we should hear about the changes in Europe. It's a time of critical changes, as it is here,' said the eminence, 'so I've asked a few people who can enlighten us. Not officials or government representatives. They have to be careful what they say. These are men of influence whose opinions matter and are not afraid to speak out. There's a film-maker and an art dealer, a jeweller and others as you will see.'

The doors of the spacious room opened outward to the verandah. A light rain sprinkled the garden and washed the dust off grass and trees. 'Here we can relax and talk informally,' he continued, 'From our side your contribution will be especially valuable. Your book has got to the heart of the question of change when you say that lasting societal change will need an altogether new mindset.'

The Master Mind's name was Mirajkar and it was well known he was an eccentric who preferred to do things his own way, more or less invisibly, influence being most effective when least seen. He was fifty and elegant, a political theorist reputed in his field and advisor to the regime in his spare time. Two of his invitees were standing on the verandah, others were arriving. Prabhakar heard French spoken, and German, and some other language.

They settled down. Sofas and armchairs had been drawn into a roomy circle for conversation. Cups of tea, pastries and sandwiches were served in a pleasant tea-time atmosphere. They were different nationalities, together here because never had Europe been so much of one mind. So said the Austrian, a publisher of children's books, who obligingly spoke first only because someone had to start. This frame of mind, he clarified—and he was certain the others would agree—was concerned about the threat to European civilization.

'As we are about the threat to ours,' put in Mirajkar like an amen, and asked him if they were taking measures to deal with the danger. Prabhakar was acquainted with the changing mood in Europe and had acquainted his students with the return of the crooked swastika, the stiff-arm salutes, the goose-stepping and its other street corner manifestations, but he had never met the Mood. Here it was, uniting Europeans as they had never been united. This is how it is and what is being done about it, he heard them say. There is a passion now evident all over Europe for an end to intrusions, nay invasions by outsiders. We must seal our borders to keep outsiders out. Keep Europe secure, keep Europe pure, keep Europe Christian, in a word, keep Europe European rolled like a refrain around the room. Prabhakar sat back in his chair, baffled and bemused. Europe had conquered the world. Europe had intruded, invaded, occupied, ruled and plundered the world. Could power and fury, power and glory, feel so besieged? There was no accounting for history's twists and turns but here was a twist of psychology. He was completely out of his depth in that realm.

He listened to the action being taken by the Mood: graffiti and flyers and leaflets to warn the public of present danger, parades carrying the swastika to keep their presence in the public eye, and public meetings to rally the like-minded. The mood is ripe. There is a response. Results will not be long coming. Meanwhile enemies of the state within the state have to be identified and dealt with along with their friends and sympathizers. Mirajkar interposed to say there could be no unity and no harmony without the removal of those who conspire against it. The Swede, or was he a German, wryly suggested putting muscular men in charge of that operation as had been done so successfully in the 1930s. There was no denying that muscled men left an indelible impression on people's minds.

And on their bodies, thought Prabhakar. But judging by what he was hearing, all this street fervour was still in the street. It had not yet entered bedrooms and kitchens. The time had not yet come for today's Europeans to talk in whispers, keep their curtains drawn and their doors locked. The time had not come to go into hiding or try in desperation to escape, as their parents had had to do. He hoped it never would. He stared at the man who was starting to speak. His head was shaved up the sides and back of his scalp, leaving a half inch of bristly hair upright on top. In his halting English he was saying the Slovenska Pospolitost, the Togetherness Movement in Slovakia, had results to show. Fourteen of their members had been elected to Parliament. In Slovakia the hour of fascist revival is already here.

'Two hundred of we Slovaks went in procession to lay flowers at the grave of our wartime leader, Jozef Tiso, in Bratislava, him who the Allies hanged as a war criminal in 1947. This was the murder of our national hero. But now it is we who decide who is criminal, who is hero. Now we remind our people of the better times we had under him. At his statue we made a vow to him. We said—as you can see it is written below this picture what we said—"You are ours and we will forever be yours."'

He passed around a photograph of the event. He and the other leaders of the procession were dressed alike in black suits, white shirts and red ties, and they all had the hairstyle. The silence in the room was impressive.

It was not possible for Prabhakar to get up and leave. Mirajkar was asking him to tell our European friends about his book, which they had not had an opportunity to read but they would be gifted copies of it. He pointed to the copies lying gift-wrapped in silver paper and red-ribboned on a table outside the circle. Prabhakar sat up. Telling them about the book was what, he supposed, he had been invited here to do. His book, he said, had been a flight of imagination, not changes he was advocating. It was an intellectual fling of his own invention. It was the kind of fling he indulged in when he wanted, well, a holiday from the classroom and from the rigours of academic discipline. It had come about because he had wondered what it would take to bring a complete about-turn in a society's ways of thinking—using his own society as an example, of course—and had reasoned that it would have to take the direct opposite of the ideas and images society had been taught to respect and revere: hallowed images like the Buddha deep in meditation, the Edicts of Ashoka preaching peace and righteousness, and in our own time the familiar figure of Gandhi, which was inseparable in people's minds from non-violence. These would have to be done away with, wiped out, dug out and destroyed wherever they were found, in books, paintings, sculptures and road names, on roadsides, in museums, wherever, so that they would be cast out of individual and collective memory. The virtues they now represent—renunciation, repentance, compassion—would be forgotten. These very words would disappear from vocabulary and any remaining rags of that inheritance would be despised as effeminate and degenerate. To excavate a society out of its age-old moorings and remake it, ruthless measures would have to be taken.

'Do go on,' Mirajkar urged, noting interest and absorption around the circle of listeners.

Prabhakar went on to say it could be done. In a manner of speaking Sparta had done it in BC by abolishing childhood. Six- and seven-year-olds had been removed from home to barracks to be schooled in war till they were eighteen. It was a martial upbringing teaching them that defeat in war would not be tolerated. Come back with your shield or on it, they were taught. So in a way it was an end to the time long associated with mother love and mother care. The children were kept barefoot and barebodied in punishing conditions to harden them to pain and privation. The result? Spartans had become the fiercest fighting force of their day. A little ripple of applause came from the circle. Mirajkar waited, then said gravely that the example of Sparta was a fascinating historical example. He was sure they would all agree it was now a time for bold initiatives, for strong men to take the lead, and forceful new images to replace tired old ones. Prabhakar's book had shown the way. Prabhakar interrupted to correct that impression but the party was over and the Europeans were saying their goodbyes.

Mirajkar was at the door seeing them off. He detained Prabhakar to ask if he was related to the

Prabhakar who was their late great founder and fountainhead of their thinking.

'No, I'm no relation.'

'Is that so? I was sure I was not mistaken. The originality and boldness of your argument—you don't mince words and you are not afraid to shock—all this being so similar points to a familial way of thought. I was even sure I saw a facial resemblance.' He smiled, 'Oh well, at any rate you are, as I myself am, from the same native earth as our revered founder.'

As Prabhakar was taking his leave, Mirajkar said, 'I don't know why a man of your intellectual calibre shouldn't be one of our policy group.'

Prabhakar excused himself. His teaching and writing took all his time.

'I understand. And we need our best minds in the universities to purge them of Communist and other atheist teachings.'

Of his childhood, Prabhakar had few actual memories. The rest of his background he had put together through his reading and research. It was factual reliable information that gave him a fairly good idea of the background he was seeking, but it was the bits he himself remembered that were the living link, the beyond-doubt connection with his lost past. He clearly remembered brick dust. It rose and fell in thick gritty gusts from the back-breaking brickload being hauled onto his father's bent-over back and carried far off by him to be unloaded on a mountain of bricks piled high for use. Brick dust drifted, veering windward from the mile-high top of the building under construction. It drifted down into hair, eyes, fingernails and toenails on the ground. It got coughed up, sneezed out, spat out.

He remembered squinting up the dizzying height where his father's naked toes gripped the bamboo scaffolding. Far below he and his barefoot playmates played catch-me, learning to dodge rusty nails and screws, iron filings and other wounding rubble. There was an open ditch they shat into, a tap in the open for drinking, washing and bathing when water came and before it suddenly went. He remembered the tin sheeting of the shed he and his family lived in. It roared and rattled when rain beat on it and when the sun scorched the sky it burned like fire. They had left that tin shed behind for this tin shed on this new construction site. Prabhakar read that poverty drove workers, the ones classed as unskilled, from their homes and made migrants of them in search of mazdoori for a living wage. Mostly they were hired where hard labour was in demand over and under the ground, in sewers and on roads, highways and building sites where they cleared and cleaned the ground, dug ditches, mixed concrete, hauled loads, erected scaffolding, picked their way skyward, and plastered and painted what they had built. If these were not skills, what were they? What was the meaning of the word? thought Prabhakar. These were skills that had to be learned untaught and untrained. They were learned the hard way, on the job. There was no regulated count of the bricks piled on your back or consideration of the weight your back could carry without breaking. No course taught what load you could jog with without losing your balance, or how to climb up a scaffolding toehold by toehold. No teacher warned: This is how, or you will fall to your death.

A study he read said there were no canteens, no toilets, and no drinking water on sites, no shoes, no helmets, no safety precautions. No crèches for babies, no care for the young who roamed where they liked unattended. The list of 'noes' went on and on: no contract, so there was nothing in writing. No eight-hour day. Work hours were elastic, uncounted and stretchable to as long as eleven per day. Workers were paid or underpaid or late paid, and unpaid for overtime. There were laws but the commonest law seemed to be the builder's bounty: fortified cane or bamboo underfoot, or only as sturdy as it came from the tree; platforms to stand on at towering heights, or none. It all depended. It sounded as if what the study called the bulk of the workforce lived or died as luck would have it. What must it have been like to work in such conditions? What inbuilt fortitude made it possible?

The nomads his parents had been remained anonymous and untraceable. He had only known them as Ma and Pitu and his grandmother as

Nannu. That was all he knew about the three who were his family and all he would ever know, there being nothing in writing to trace them by. Nomads have no address. Illiterates leave no trail.

There were other remembered scraps: the stranger who came and joined their catch-me. He pulled funny faces, wiggled his ears and twitched his nose, making them roll about laughing. He swung them around by their arms and took them piggy-back riding, galloping them turn by turn round and round the site and up the road and back, and galloping away with one of them. They never saw their playmate, or the stranger, again.

He must have been four or five years old when the windstorm started whirling brick dust in circles, thrashing treetops and whirling one treetop off its tree at the edge of the site. The wind gathered fury. The bamboo bent and his father's foot lost its grip. He saw his father's leg swing out helpless, frantic for a foothold, his flailing arm finding no handhold, his body hurtling down to hit the ground headfirst. An avalanche of loosened bricks thundered down on his mother who squatted below, her hand shielding the rotis she had brought for him. The wind swallowed his own wild wails. The storm brought his grandmother out of the tin shed.

On some day after that Nannu took him to the 'bhaktin ischool' which was not a school but a refuge run by the bhaktins of the Kolkata Mother who had set up rescue homes like this in other cities and whose bhaktins picked up the diseased and dying from gutters to let them die in dignity on beds. Nannu didn't leave him on the doorstep, trusting he might be taken in as some newborns and other unwanteds had been according to those who knew. She sat herself down on the steps to wait—for how long he never knew—and sat him on the step below her, locked between her spindly legs. Dry-eyed but distraught and hoarse from loud mourning she made the situation as audible as she could in words, and with ample gestures when words failed, to the bhaktin who opened the door, informing her she was committing the boy huddled at her feet to the bhaktin's care: this child of her daughter who was killed by brick thunder when her husband's death-fall split his skull open at her feet. Nannu bent and put a finger on his mouth and then on her own to make it doubly clear that the child was mute. He had not spoken since the bamboo bent and the bricks thundered down, not eaten, not slept. The bhaktin, who till then must have assumed the crumpled motionless heap on the doorstep must be ill from natural causes, made a sign like a cross over herself.

What had become of his grandmother after that and where she went Prabhakar would never know. He devoutly hoped she had made her way back to the home before migration and wished she could have heard him speak again as shock dimmed and utmost horror receded into some crevice of consciousness where it got stored like broken furniture in an attic. He attributed the return of his voice to the statue in the chapel, a figure of grace and sweet, surpassing gentleness, though he knew none of these words at the time, only the feelings her figure stirred in him. She wore a long blue robe. Her head was covered. Her eyes were cast down. Her arms hung by her sides with her palms turned a little outward. He had been told she interceded with higher authority for those who needed help because she had borne unbearable sorrow, and seen and suffered indescribable pain. Her presence reached out and enfolded him. One day he spoke. At night he slept.

He learned to read and write and read and read. He ate hungrily and as avidly devoured all that school could teach him, in the Catholic school run by their church that the bhaktins later sent him to. The day came when his schoolmaster in senior school told him he had been admitted to college and would need a surname. Prabhu didn't know where he came from, which would indicate the name with the name-ending he should have, so the master tried hard to think of a name, any name that would go with Prabhu. He came up with one that sounded something like it, hoping it might be easier for the boy to remember. Memorize it, he instructed, don't forget it. It's your name. And Prabhu Prabhakar he had been ever since. Prabhakar was how he thought of himself and the person he had become, though he was Prabhu to his friends.

They ordered their favourite brain masala at the dhaba that had expanded and now called itself a café, written 'kaif' in Hindi, and known as kaif to its customers. It had added a low rung of office workers to its working class clientele and a plastic menu of 'continental' choices. The time-honoured age-old irreplaceables were down at the bottom of the menu. Fortunately progress had not affected the brain masala, or the gular kebabs they could get nowhere else, or the rumali rotis that Rafeeq, the cook, made at their request. Prabhakar and Rahman went there for lunch when they wanted to catch up. It was far enough from the university to avoid meeting the VC's busybodies and their favourite as far as food was concerned.

'What was it all about? How did it go?' Rahman asked and Prabhakar described the tea party.

'For some reason Europeans feel they're under siege, and the Master Mind thinks we're under siege here. I kept wondering if I was hearing right. Why was I invited?'

'You wrote a book,' said Rahman.

He signalled a server for more of everything.

'You must be the last innocent left if you think a book is just a book. As it happens, and as you are always prompt to point out, you're not the first person to have written this kind of book.'

'What kind?' Prabhakar's bewilderment was complete.

'A terrifying story like no other. Mary Shelley wrote one two hundred years ago,' said Rahman.

Prabhakar had not heard of it. He waited for more.

'She wrote a novel in which a science professor called Frankenstein creates a grotesque uncontrollable monster out of chemicals and human remains. That's what you've done, Prabhu. You've written a story in which good and evil change places. You've created a monstrous scenario.'

Prabhakar brushed that aside impatiently. 'But it's a fantasy, Rahman, it's an exercise of my imagination. You know that. I was spinning a yarn.'

'So was Mary Shelley. Only her yarn stayed on paper. Yours might not.'

'Good God, that would be a nightmare.'

'It would.'

They paid their bill and went out behind the kaif to the kitchen to pay their customary homage to Rafeeq, and give him a small token of their appreciation for their feast. Rafeeq threw up his floury hands in resignation, indicating his shrunken domain, now that it was shared with the 'continental' cook.

The following day it became official. Bharat was no longer Mata. From now on Bharat was Pitrubhumi. Fatherland. And from now on females above the age of seventeen would be addressed as Devi as a mark of respect in a culture which revered women.

Francois and Prahlad had a wide and varied acquaintance. It was at Francois's that Prabhakar had met Lisette. Named after, she was telling someone, her grandmother's favourite Maurice Chevalier song. She sang a line of it: 'Eyes of Lisette, the smile of Mignonette, the sweetness of Suzette, in you array...'

She was attractive in her unaffected spontaneity. 'What's the rest of the song?' Prabhakar asked.

'Grace of Delphine, the charm of Josephine...' She laughed. 'Oh, I can't remember the rest of it but it ends with "You are my ideal, my love parade." *Love Parade* was the name of the movie it was in.'

She was called away and disappeared from view. Her foreignness and air of sophistication kept him from seeking her out again. But after a while a pleasant surprise. She was back with a drink in her hand and sat down in a chair next to his to talk to him. About a business matter, it turned out. She was in India to look into the food scene, not for Michelin—there were other respected connoisseurs who gave star status to restaurants—and she was going to be touring around investigating on behalf of one of them. But could he suggest any outstanding place here before she went south? Francois and Prahlad's Bonjour with its accent on peace and quiet at breakfast, its delicious offerings and its lovely Indo-French ambience had been a discovery. And what darling people they both were. Yes, her assignment would include the people who owned and ran the places. It made for an all-round picture. Could he suggest any places?

Prabhakar had never heard of Michelin (or for that matter of Maurice Chevalier) and wanted to say he didn't eat out much, it was too expensive, so he was the wrong person to ask. Then, suddenly annoyed with himself for holding back on the diet of emperors—what a betrayal—he said he did know a place.

'Oh, wonderful! I'll write down the name and address.'

'It doesn't have an address. It would be hard for you to find, it's off a road in an alley. If you like I could take you there.'

'Would you? If it's not too much trouble? I'm intrigued.'

He regretted his offer immediately—it was impossible to picture her in the kaif—but now it was made. On the appointed day, a day of sullen heat, he drove her through the bazaar traffic of cars, strolling cows, buffalos and three-wheelers, off the main road and down the alley to the kaif. It was lunchtime and crowded. Fast fans whirled the stagnant air high above them. They found an empty table under a fan in the middle of the lunchtime clamour. A server swung his jharan off his shoulder, wiped spilled water and some sticky stuff, flicked a blob of chutney off the table and swung the jharan back on. Lisette mopped her forehead with her handkerchief and looked around.

'This is more like it,' she said, 'Something a bit different.'

Prabhakar had forgotten the true researcher's obsession with research. He ordered lavishly and with care.

'I'm familiar with Indian food,' she assured him while they waited, 'Curry is very popular at home.'

'Curry? Which Indian food are you familiar with?'

'What d'you mean, which?' Light dawned. 'I see. Of course. How absurd of me. It's as if I'd lumped smorgasbord with ravioli.'

'Exactly,' approved Prabhakar. 'We'll be eating Mughal.'

Later, ignoring the trickle of sweat streaking down her cheek, she was concentrating on what she was eating, 'Great gourmets those Mughals must have been. It's impossible to guess what spices have gone into this, it's such an amazing blend of so many flavours.' A little later, halfway through the meal, she was astonished by the taste and texture of the kebab she had bitten into. 'I've never eaten a kebab like this, it's pure silk, and who would have thought of putting shredded orange of all things into a kebab! I would never have believed it.'

'This particular kebab was invented for a toothless old Nawab so it had to be soft as silk. The royal khansamas were experimenters. They had to be, to produce new delights to please royal palates.'

'Or get their heads cut off?'

'No, nothing of the sort, they were far too valuable. And they probably ate the same food, plenty of leftovers. As far as that's concerned Islam has no big divide between master and servant.'

'I can't thank you enough for bringing me here,' said Lisette after her heartfelt appreciation—hand on heart—had been translated to Rafeeq in the kitchen, and he, squatted among a clutter of utensils, had responded as graciously, hand to brow.

She was still under the spell of Rafeeq's cooking on the way to her hotel. 'And to think he does all this in that tiny space, in that heat, with no machines to mince and grind and blend, only that helper. The man is a magician. And what about all those recipes? They're obviously in his head. But where d'you think they originated? Along the crossroads between Europe and Asia? In Persia and Arabia and Arabian Nights places to land up here and become Indian?'

Prabhakar had not thought of gular kebab and rogan josh in those romantic terms, taking it for granted that most things Indian were mixtures of here and elsewhere. He said it was the same with music, dance, language and a hundred other things. But Lisette was intent on what she had eaten and a write-up that would be her most original, featuring Rafeeq, and not the kaif's owner, as the person who mattered in the kaif.

'You've been so kind,' she said, 'I'd never have known about this place but for you. Can't I give you a cup of tea at my hotel?'

She agreed to have it at his place instead, where

she pottered around his bookshelves while he made it, spotted his book about fashion, sat down with it, and asked if she could borrow it. She would take it to read on her food travels over the next couple of weeks, she said, but would come over before she left for London to say goodbye and return his book.

'There's no need to return it, Lisette, please keep it.'

Over tea, 'You've never married, Prabhu?' she asked, not inquisitively. She was enquiring in her usual keenly interested fashion.

'No. Marriage among us needs antecedents. Background, family, uncles and aunts, all that paraphernalia. My parents died when I was a child and I have no relations.'

'None? Not one?' She considered that, absorbing—or so it seemed to him—the consequences of that lifelong deprivation.

She came anyway to say goodbye, saying she knew him much better after reading his book and had enjoyed Josephine's amorous goings-on. What a fun way to look at history and such fun to read, like Ten Sixty-Six.

Prabhakar told her it had been fun to write.

It wasn't very sporting of Bonaparte to desert Josephine, she said, considering his own Polish affair with Marie Walenska, not to mention his child by her.

'But I'm sure you know, Prabhu, that was why he had to tear himself away from Josephine. She couldn't have a baby, and as he was going royal, he had to have a legitimate son.'

'Yes, I do know. That's a fact of history. But all that muslin must have given him a good excuse, don't you think?'

'I'm sure it did!' she laughed.

She had brought her write-up about the kaif for him to read. It described accurately what she had eaten, with some history and geography thrown in: food that had journeyed, linking far-apart cultures, transporting robust feasts of flesh and fowl along with delicate creations of spun sugar and syrups, wafting flavours and aromas across borders to become native to wherever they were eaten, and for Mughal to become forever Indian. This conclusion marked her in Prabhakar's eyes as someone distinct and discerning, as down-to-earth as she was romantic, and never confusing the two. He had not expected her to remember his remarks about assimilation or to take them seriously.

There followed a description of Rafeeq's work space cluttered with gas cylinders and brass cookware, its odours of garlic and cloves, its mountain of potato, onion and ginger peel, and the splutter of hot oil where mutton sizzled in a redolence of spices. From this cubbyhole of a kitchen had come the magical meal she had eaten. Her last sentence caught Prabhakar unprepared. It crowned Rafeeq with 'a skill that defied working conditions'. For Prabhakar it was the highest accolade that could be bestowed on one of the millions who laboured unheard and unseen.

Time and distance had put him beyond the reach of unmanageable sorrow. What had taken its place was a silent seething anger against those who turned a blind eye to skill. They must be the grossest among humankind who did not know skill when they saw it and made use of it, and for whom human life was expendable and cheaply replaceable. He got up and gave the pages back to Lisette and thanked her fervently for her understanding. She could not have known what he was thanking her for or what was going through his mind but she seemed to understand its emotional importance. She hugged him impulsively and said they must keep in touch.

A week after the Wednesday which was the day she had not shown up, Prabhakar found time to look for the bunch of newspaper clippings of the trial a few months ago that he had put away among his files. No trial could take place for want of evidence, they had said. The dead could not be questioned and no survivor had come forward, no eyewitness, nobody. Told-to accounts after the event could not be taken as evidence. But the noise about it would not go away. And then she had come forward.

She refused a lawyer—who could afford a lawyer? She and her colleagues certainly couldn't. She said she would speak for herself. She asked the judge the regime had chosen to head the enquiry commission they had set up, to guide her in procedure as she was ignorant of it and did not want to disrespect it in any way. Asked what organization she belonged to, she said none. None? Then with what authority and under whose auspices had she come forward?

'On our own. We're a voluntary group, Your Honour, myself and four other women from different countries who've seen what massacres did to women in Serbia, Bosnia and Rwanda. We came together to find out what was happening here and we divided the affected areas among ourselves.'

So hers was an eyewitness account? Yes, she had been there at the time. She had been in the village she had been allotted, where most of the families were Muslim.

The clipping said the judge could barely conceal his impatience. If she had been there at the time, why had she not come forward then? Her brief reply was hardly heard and he must have decided not to pursue that point because she had gone on without pause or preamble to say: It was still daylight when the mob came...

Came where? Be specific, from the judge. Name

of village given, she went back to the beginning:
It was still daylight when the mob came yelling—
yelling their war cry... and threw lighted branches
around to set the village on fire. Families rushed
out of their homes and ran in every direction into
the fields. The mob ran after them. And after us: me
and three of the village women and their children.
The wheat had been cut and we kept stumbling on
the stubble until the woman who was very pregnant
could go no further. They caught us and beat our
legs with iron rods and forced us to the ground.

The clipping said she spoke in an expressionless
monotone. The thought of it gripped Prabhakar,
as it had the first time he had read the account.
It conjured a cultivated deadness and eyes glazed
with unsheddable tears. Had she dulled her voice
to mesmerize herself into a somnolent state so that
she could speak the unspeakable? She was told to
speak up. Her voice rose: I said they beat our legs
with rods and forced us to the ground...

The judge ordered silence or he would have the
court cleared. He would have ordered a separate
room for her testimony but she refused and said

it must be heard, and continued: They pulled our clothes off. More men came. They dragged us apart to make room and kicked our legs apart. Each of us was surrounded and held down...

Prabhakar could not go on. The sentence hit him harder than it had when he first read it. Now that he had met her, he saw her surrounded and forced down. He knew he must reread the rest of it but it would have to be later. His immediate need was to meet her and offer her his support in whatever way. There had been no chance to talk to her at Francois's and now it was an anguished necessity. Too much time, a whole week, had been lost. He rang Francois for her telephone number and Francois said wait a minute and gave him the address as well. He dialled the number, heard it go on ringing, six, eight, more times. The next thing he knew he was on his way.

The house was in a quiet corner of a shady lane and if there had once been a name on the gate, it was no longer there. The high wall on either side of the gate was embedded with jagged broken glass. The short path to the house was hedge-lined and unevenly pebbled—it would be rough on shoe soles and hard on tyres—to discourage visitors? He bumped his car up the drive. The front verandah was curtained off by low-hanging bougainvillea. A house in purdah.

He was admitted to a room whose furniture was minimalist and geometrical, all straight lines and sharp corners. Not intended for lounging. Flamboyance lined one wall in a painting of war-like shapes in a blaze of discordant colours by a famous painter of a massacre during the exodus of the Partition. The polished floor had scattered rugs that he could not help describing to himself as woven of bleeding red and bitter orange. A stark room that said, state your business and go. He had not planned what to say and he had no idea how he would explain his presence. He remained standing.

A door behind him opened and closed. He turned around to see she had come in. She was all in white, white cotton sari and a white sleeveless choli that forced his attention to a raw-looking ugly patchwork of ridged scars along her naked upper arm. The repellent sight made him go swiftly to her and hardly realizing it, put his arms around her.

His shock was immense when she gave a strangled scream of a cry and broke violently free of him. Striving for composure, she sat down, motioned him to a chair and covered her face with her hands.

When she raised her head she said matter-of-factly, 'It was the contact. I can't manage physical contact, any kind, any more.'

The enormity of what she had said, and left unsaid, kept him from saying anything at all. It was the difference, the great void between reading about it and seeing it for oneself. He grappled with her problem. There were times that called for the crutch of religion. He didn't know if that crutch was available to her. He had none to offer—he had no religion other than reason—but the scripture of his childhood had been Christian and it had been awash with miracles. The miracle of the loaves and fishes, water miraculously made wine and most miraculous of all the command to a corpse to get up and walk, which the corpse obeyed. Lazarus stood up and walked as if he had never been dead. Nothing less than a miracle of that drastic order would restore her fully to the world of the living.

Her 'Will you have a cup of coffee?' eased the high tension.

She remembered meeting him at Francois's. She had not been able to let him know she couldn't come last Wednesday because he had not given her his phone number. The coffee was hot, strong and reviving, a painkiller of a kind. The atmosphere scaled down to nearly normal. She had spoken frankly and unsparingly about herself, and this allowed him to be as plainspoken, telling her he knew about her ordeal because he had read the evidence she had given at the trial. Would she look upon him as a friend, could they meet and talk, could he take her out occasionally, getting out and about would surely help. A puzzled look greeted his proposal. This was what she was doing, getting out and about. That's how they had happened to meet. In fact, meeting people and being sociable had been prescribed as therapy and the psychiatrist had called it a necessary part of her treatment after her abortion and her stay in hospital for other damages. She had been doing as prescribed, as well as getting on with writing her report. But, yes, it would be nice to meet. The report? She and her colleagues were writing their accounts of the areas they had been assigned as well as their own earlier personal experiences and these were going to be published as a book. By a feminist press abroad as the new law about womanly modesty would ban its publication here.

He asked, hardly daring to, but horribly aware of her butchered arm, if her injuries had healed as far as possible. The outer ones had healed, yes, but as he could see they had left their permanent reminder. It was policy—decided by herself and two of her colleagues who had been raped in other such wars—to leave their outer wounds exposed. Rape had been hidden and talk about it forbidden for too long. And besides, she, who for some reason fate had let live, had a duty to her tortured and slaughtered companions and their little children, and must let her wounds speak for them.

She offered him more coffee. Frank and forthcoming though she had been—a matter of policy as she called it—she had kept off any mention of her invisible wounds and the interior havoc of rape that made a human touch unendurable. He knew that trespass into that zone would not be permitted. He understood as if she had said it that the frigid wasteland she now inhabited was one she must find her way out of alone. But yes, she had acknowledged that life did have to go on.

At home that night he knew he must finish reading her testimony before he met her again, this time with greater attention, to understand what she had been through and what he was up against if he was going to be of any real help to her. He spread the press clippings on his dining table, weighted them down and continued from where he had left off:

They pulled our clothes off. The youngest of us, she was a beautiful young girl, fought them, shouting and struggling against being stripped naked so they cut off her breasts to silence her. The pregnant woman was on one side of me. They kept hitting her swollen belly, beating it to abort the foetus before they got onto her one by one. The waiting men laughed and egged them on, showing their own penises and kept yelling, 'Now we will make little Hindus inside you.' One of them picked up the woman's son, threw him face down and forced himself into the boy, telling the child, 'Without castor oil in your arse we will make you holler.' You see, Your Honour, she said in the same expressionless monotone, looking up from the paper from which she had been reading, their voices were much louder than our cries—they wanted to make sure we heard them—that is why I have been able to read you their exact words. Above us we heard them say 'Use them as much as you can, don't let a single one go.' Not even the three-month-old baby that one man picked up and smashed on the stubble. The woman on my other side begged for mercy for her two little girls but they took the two terrified little children and raped them in front of their mother, and then her in front of them…

All this while there was no silencing order from the judge. None needed. The exact words had produced a rapt silence. She put down her paper.

'About me, Your Honour,' she continued in the same monotone, 'Two men dragged my arms up. A third one grabbed my breasts and clawed and scratched them with his nails while the fourth man was raping me. Then more men came, eight more. And raped me one by one. Nine of them altogether. On the other women I cannot say how many, I could hear nothing, see nothing any more... When they were done with me one of them found a rod they had beaten our legs with and hit me with it, on my stomach and my body all over. I was dead to pain by then and I must have lost consciousness because they took me for dead, after making sure with the rod that I was... By then they must have been in a hurry to go. When I came to, it was growing dark and they had gone. I tried to move, I tried to get on all fours to crawl, to look for my companions, but I couldn't move. I could only turn my head to one side and I saw thick black smoke coming from a fire the men had lit some way off. It told me that was where my companions were, thrown in to hasten the process because they were taking too long to die... I don't know how long I lay there till two of my colleagues came looking for me... took me away...'

The judge's grave conclusion: A most unfortunate event, most condemnable. And that it should happen to one in your position... The work of unknown miscreants. Best forgotten.

Prabhakar assembled the clippings in a neat pile and laid them back in their file. He got up and put the file back in its place in the steel chest of drawers he had taken it from. It was imperative to stay cool and rational. Life after rape was his problem now, not hers alone. And there was no such thing as a modern miracle.

No miracles, he reflected, yet there had been inexplicable events. Not quite the same thing, but he had come across a compelling one a year ago when he was preparing a lecture he was to deliver on Gandhi. It had happened to an American journalist. Prabhakar took Vincent Sheean's book from his Gandhi bookshelf to refresh his memory. He had found the book absorbing. Foreign correspondents were a breed whose forte was facts, not unexplained and unexplainable events. Sheean himself was known for his wide coverage of the brute facts of the twentieth century: the rise of fascism in Europe in the 1930s, the Spanish Civil War and the Second World War. He had met and reported on every wartime leader across Europe and Asia. And then he met Gandhi.

Prabhakar opened Sheean's book to the part that led up to the unexplained event. He had come to India and met Gandhi, had long talks with him and travelled with him to understand the workings of a political mind whose war without violence had made world news. Bizarre the command he had given his weaponless army of followers: If blood must be shed in this battle, let it be your own. Unheard of his political philosophy that had nothing to do with politics but began and ended with what had to be done for those whom he called the last and the least. Sheean had never met such a personality in politics, and he had met everyone of consequence. The meaning of his encounter with Gandhi became stupefyingly clear in his powerful description of what he went through on the evening of the 30th of January 1948:

He was in the garden of Birla House at five o'clock on 'one of those shining Delhi evenings' along with other foreign correspondents and the people of Delhi streaming into the garden for the daily prayer meeting. 'I felt well and happy and grateful to be here,' wrote Sheean. About ten feet away, Gandhi, with a shawl covering his bare chest against the chill, was making his way slowly through the garden, across the lawn from where Sheean and other newspaper men were standing, to go up the four or five steps that led to the prayer ground. Then came 'four small, dull, dark explosions.'

'What followed must be told as it happened,' wrote Sheean, '(to ME, ME) or there is no truth in it.' Prabhakar read Sheean's account of what followed those explosions decades ago. It was still painful to read and still profoundly moving: 'Inside my own head there occurred a wave-like disturbance which I can only compare to a storm at sea—wind and wave surging tremendously back and forth...' Sheean had leaned forward from the brick wall he was standing against, doubled up and 'bent almost in two.'

'I felt the consciousness of the Mahatma leave me then—I know of no other way of expressing this: he left me. The storm inside my head continued...'

At the same time he became aware of a burning

stinging sensation in the fingers of his right hand, and tears unlike tears, that were more like acid burning his eyes. When he was able to look at his fingers he saw blisters on the third and fourth fingers of his right hand. They were filled with water. There had been no blisters before he heard the shots.

What flooded into Sheean's mind as he described this discovery was the 'many many' dreams he had had night after night the summer before in Vermont, dreams of trying frantically, and failing utterly, to thrust his body, his arm, his leg, any part of himself between Gandhi and his inevitable murder. He kept reliving his desperate dream-efforts to shield Gandhi and be killed in his place so that Gandhi would live. For days after the assassination in Delhi he was obsessed by the horror and agony of his failure 'to die for the Mahatma, the last best hope of earth.'

The blisters—would they be stigmata? Prabhakar looked up stigmata. His dictionary called it 'marks resembling wounds on crucified body of Christ'. Sheean made no such exalted claim. Days later, when he could at last function normally, he concluded that the blisters, which had appeared the instant the shots were fired, were 'a psychosomatic phenomenon', by no means new to science. Psychosomatic, Prabhakar confirmed, meant 'resulting from interaction of mind and body, or influence of one on the other.' Sheean had accepted this scientific explanation but it had not replaced his conviction that the blisters were proof of his connection with the murder he had forseen in his dreams and his calamitous failure to prevent it, in reality as in his dreams.

Explain them how you will, there are still and always will be wonders that will amaze us. It was an idea Prabhakar would have liked to discuss with her. In love there is a longing to share. What did the beloved think of Sheean's remarkable experience? What would she think of the Iranian film he had seen a week ago or the spy thriller he was reading? How had she reacted to the election in Nepal? Much as he longed to make love to her, he longed as much to know her in all the ways that make for discoveries between two people. She herself had said life had to go on.

He had learned about sex the way one does, gaining knowledge and experience as one goes along. Love had not needed learning. He had known it since birth. In a remembered scrap of memory he lay between the two who loved each other. He grew from birth to infant to child lying in the small narrow space between their bodies every night. When they thought he had fallen asleep he would be shifted aside with tender care, letting them reach for the comfort of each other after the hard, heavy day spent apart. Their sighs and murmurs assured him they had found each other, and he could fall asleep knowing they were where they belonged, inseparably joined. At some moment of remembrance long after he had lost them he had come to believe that if it had to happen, it was more merciful this way, for neither of his parents could have lived without the other.

Prabhakar tried to decide what kind of film he could take her to that would interest and entertain her, take her mind off what had happened if only for an hour or two. At this point he was not even sure they would ever meet again though she had seemed willing. But this came about not long afterwards.

❧

Prabhakar and Rahman were going to the kaif for lunch and took Lopez who had never been. In high anticipation of the meal they had promised him, they ordered. The server looked helpless. The owner was sent for, arrived, jammed his palms together, and stood there in harassed pleading posture before two valued customers and a third esteemed guest. He apologized in a lowered voice. Rafeeq away, no Mughal. It was irritating, but it was too late to go somewhere else so they settled dejectedly for hamburgers. The plastic menu informed them these would be chicken in the bun, no longer mutton, the real thing.

Lopez reminded his friends: no meat unless proven to be mutton, not cow. The Cow Comission went around making sure. He was thinking of becoming a vegetarian himself, he was scared as hell that his fridge might be raided and the mutton turned into beef. Suspects were being dealt with out on the streets, surrounded by cameras and cheering beholders. He didn't fancy that treatment for himself.

It was far from reassuring in view of Rafeeq's disappearance or dismissal. They drank their cloying Limcas, not sure how to find out about Rafeeq. The kaif's water wasn't safe and there was no mineral water left. All the bottles of mineral water had been commandeered by 'them', the 'they' and 'them' who came and went, mysteriously unnamed.

Lopez, who taught Modern Europe, said, 'This tea party you were at, Prabhu, you said the Slovak was well ahead of the others.'

'Why wouldn't he be? They've had practice. They had a flourishing Nazi republic during the war, with a Gestapo and Jew-disposal and all the trimmings, and evidently there's a tremendous nostalgia for those good old days when everybody was kept in line, or in harmony, as they called it. Togetherness was the watchword. Not that the other speakers weren't harking back to the glories of the 1930s, but I did get the feeling that some of them were sitting back and waiting to see which way the wind would blow before they risked investing in it. Only fools rush in. Compared with the rest of them the Slovak was the only Boy Scout.'

'But most people are little people who have to go along with whatever's happening,' said Lopez, 'either because they don't know any better, or they have no choice and can't afford to lose their wages or their lives.'

'Most people,' repeated Prabhakar, and again with stubborn emphasis, 'most people everywhere, in Europe or here or anywhere else, only ask to be left in peace to live their lives. It doesn't seem too much to ask.'

Rahman broke in on their reflections on the rise and rise of fascism. 'Look here, Prabhu, we must go and see Rafeeq as soon as possible. He'll be in need of work and help, poor man.'

He lifted a hand to signal to the owner, who came. No, the owner did not know where Rafeeq lived. The server who arrived to remove their plates of half-eaten chickenburgers did know and told them, after darting a look right and left.

∾

Prahlad had told Sergei he was going to dance for a special occasion and Sergei thought it was typical of him to return to his art for the occasion. It would be his way of celebrating what must be the first or the second anniversary of Bonjour. The party was to be at Francois's apartment which was larger than his own. Their other friends were already there when Sergei arrived, sitting on cushions on the carpet in a room that had been cleared of furniture. A hypnotic tabla beat sounded from the shining floor beyond the carpet, against the sliding sound of strings being tuned. A sofa had been left at the back of the room for those who were unused to the floor and Sergei who had come in late sat down there. He was feeling like a drink but no drinks were on offer, which confirmed his impression that Prahlad did not believe in disturbing or diluting effects. This, he guessed with some amusement, must be a personality trait, and had nothing to do with any highbrow conception of art. Prahlad had even taken care not to disturb Sergei's breakfast, letting him eat his Eggs Benedict in peace before coming to talk to him.

Sergei listened to the leisurely tuning of the two instruments to the perfection required. He found it curious, this display of making ready in front of an assembled audience, instead of appearing with tuned instruments ready to perform. Could it be that involving the audience in the tuning up was a traditional part of the performance, a way of involving the audience from beginning to end, like saying: We are one, united, not separated, by Art. Be with us, not way out there. There was a suggestion of that in the seating arrangement that had artists and audience at the same level, all on the floor. It was far removed from a concert in the West which is sacrosanct unto itself, brilliantly illuminated onstage and cut off by pitch darkness below and beyond. He allowed himself to relax. It was pleasant to be thinking about matters other than work. There was no niggling worry about what might be needing his urgent attention. For many years he had flown in, and mission accomplished, flown out of countries. He had seen the sights in some but he had not felt what a much-travelled acquaintance of his called the pulse, or heard the heartbeat, of any. Now that Ivan had taken over in New York—grandson of Dimitri with the business acumen Dimitri would have been proud of—and his own capable deputy was in charge in London while he was away, he could look forward to more time to himself. Starting now.

The tuning was done, the rhythm begun, and Prahlad was dancing. He had a partner, a young woman from the troupe he had belonged to. Her embroidered bell-shaped skirt swayed from side to side, twinkling as light glanced off the tiny mirrors sewn all over it. She wore a satiny top and a headdress like a little cone with a transparent veil drifting over it. Prahlad's costume was as graceful, a dhoti that left his legs bare to the knee, and a green satin or velvet waistcoat. Their movements were small, subtle and sinuous. This was not the dramatic demanding dance called kathak which Sergei had seen performed in Edinburgh, with its controlled facial expressions and gestures, its breathtaking spinning and subsiding, and the mathematical exactitude of its rhythmic footwork. Watching kathak he had been reminded, for lack of any other comparison, of Chopin's minute waltz. It was the timebound discipline of both. He mentioned this to the woman who had come in after him and sat beside him on the sofa. A comparison she would never have thought of but yes, she agreed, it was an interesting point. And of course the dance we are watching is entirely different from kathak, though this, too, is a classical dance. We have so many classical dance forms in different parts of the country, all very different from each other. This one is from the northeast, it's called Manipuri and it acts out the love story of Krishna and Radha. That's why Prahlad chose it. It's dainty and delicate, as you can see, but it has its own discipline. The beauty is in the wrist movements. Watch the fingerwork and the way the dancing feet lift off as if they've flown up. Sergei watched as directed and saw she was right. He decided Manipuri must have been created for long thin fingers like Prahlad's and bodies as light and nimble as those of the two performing artists.

It would seem so, she agreed, but she wanted Sergei to know that this performance was not pure Manipuri. Prahlad was improvising. Since he was not with his troupe any more he hadn't been able to get the drummers who would have been drumming and dancing around him and his partner, or to borrow the cymbals and the rest of the classic accompaniment.

'Being Prahlad, I think he just wanted to dance, no matter how, for this important occasion. For him there isn't any better way to celebrate. I think he must have been born dancing.'

Her voice had the warmth and affection of a caress and it made Sergei turn to smile at her. His glance jerked away. He was unable to suppress a shudder at the sight of livid reddish skin showing above her low-cut blouse. Not a skin disease. It was something incomparably worse. It looked inflicted.

She said to his averted face, 'Manipuri is from our northeast and I'm no expert but they say it has influences from the countries around us, even from as remote as Siberia. Isn't it incredible how cultures travel and blend?'

No one applauded when the dance ended. Something else seemed to be starting. The musicians took their instruments away and a silver tray was brought in, of miniature clay oil lamps—called diyas, she explained—and set down on the floor. Prahlad and Francois, dressed like Prahlad who was still in his silk and velvet Manipuri costume, came in and sat down crosslegged in front of the tray. Behind them a voice was chanting.

'The diyas are in place of the fire there should have been,' Sergei heard his neighbour say softly, 'and the mantras being chanted are the ones actually recited in the service.'

Sergei was mystified but could ask no questions—he had not got over the shock of her ravaged skin—as Prahlad and Francois got up and started stepping around the tray of diyas. They walked around it several times in single file and then out through the door into the drawing room. The floor sitters, already up, streamed after them. There was an outburst of rejoicing. Congratulations were called out amid loud laughter and the popping of champagne corks. Francois and Prahlad, bedecked with jasmine garlands someone had brought, were at the centre of it all. A cry of delight from Prahlad when he saw Sergei. He took his arm out of Francois's and made his way to him.

'You remembered, Sergei! You are a friend of the heart!'

'How could I forget, after all the breakfasts I'm enjoying at Bonjour. Is it the first or the second anniversary of Bonjour?'

Prahlad fell back, mortified. 'I didn't tell you? It is our wedding day. We have just got married!'

Francois came to them. Glasses of champagne followed.

'We couldn't have a civil marriage or get a priest to marry us,' he said, 'because our marriage is illegal, Sergei, we have broken the law. So Prahlad decided to do things his own way. He loves ceremony,' spoken like an indulgent lover.

'I'm so glad I could be here,' said Sergei sincerely. 'Let me wish you both lifelong happiness.'

They drew him into a three-cornered embrace, called for more champagne to toast each other and drank. Prahlad put his glass down, lifted his arms high and clapped his hands. Faces turned towards him. 'These are tragic times,' he announced. 'The times are grim, and so, my friends—let's dance!' This was greeted with enthusiasm and when

Francois, choosing from his Italian collection, put 'Signorina Cappucina' on the player, everyone danced, in pairs without touching or athletically on their own, unlike the intimacy of the ballroom dancing Sergei had known, with your partner held agreeably close. Those who knew the words were singing. The winsome young woman who had partnered Prahlad came to Sergei, her bell-skirt swaying, and said 'Dance?'

'I'm sorry, I wish I could but I can't,' he apologized, but she urged 'Come!' and took him firmly by the wrist. At the edge of the dancers she lifted her arms, twirled and untwirled her fingers and went into variations of Manipuri to the rhythm of 'Cappucina', leaving Sergei to devise variations of his own, which he found himself doing.

Prabhakar suddenly saw her, exquisite as ever. She was talking to Prahlad on the other side of the room. It was a gift he had least expected, and thanking whatever gods there be, he wound his way through the dancers to spend the rest of the evening with her.

The wedding buffet, laid among tall lighted candles and fresh flowers, created a hush. Francois put love and longing on the player to accompany it and beckoned his guests to the buffet as a voluptuous voice began singing his and Prahlad's favourite 'Al-di-la' in Italian and then its English version 'Beyond'.

'Beyond the most beautiful things, beyond the stars, there you are, just for me…Every star will light the way above me to where you are… Just to measure your worth I'd move heaven and earth to be near you…You're my life, you're my love, you're my Al-di-la …'

The song drew Francois and Prahlad irresistibly together in an emotional moment no one disturbed.

'Al-di-la' had its trance-like effect on the diners, which was why it had taken Sergei some time to get back to the question in his mind: What had Prahlad meant by grim and tragic times? Sergei had joined his sofa acquaintance—who he now knew was the dear friend Prahlad had wanted him to meet—and another guest at a table in a small alcove off the dining room, and was taken by surprise when she said, in Russian, that she would try to answer his question. Her mother was Russian and had named her Katerina, 'So please call me Katya as my friends do.' It accounted for the rare arresting beauty of her father's dark skin displaying her mother's green eyes and Slavic cheekbones.

There is no doubt that each language makes an impact all its own. Sergei found the impact of what she was saying more searing in his mother tongue and hers than it would have been in English. Prabhakar who knew the facts well, listened to her calm recital with deep misgiving. Could it be right to repeat and rerepeat this monstrous tale? Should pain be probed and prodded over and over again? As she went on he began reluctantly to see why she thought it necessary. If those who survive don't tell the tale, she had said, it will be forgotten. The agonies of those women and children, their pain, their horror and terror, not just mine, will never have happened unless we tell it. Telling it passes it on, makes it our heritage. It's because tales have been told and retold that we have a *Ramayana* and a *Mahabharata*. Our epic horrors are no less our heritage.

When she had completed her personal story she said Sergei should be given the larger picture, not just her bit of it, and asked Prabhakar if he would go on with the rest of it.

The haunting declaration of love that was 'Al-di-la' would have been ruled out as unsuitable background music for barbaric acts onscreen in cinema, but Prabhakar could not separate 'You're my life, you're my love' from the barbaric assaults on her body and his intense desire to rid her of that memory.

'Prabhu? Could you tell Sergei...?'

'I'm sorry, yes of course. I was wondering where to begin. I might as well start with today. I was driving to the university this morning—I go past the Gandhi statue on Mall Road...'

A statue unlike the usual standing or sitting statues of heroes in public places, he told Sergei. It was unlike the military heroes majestic on horseback, with the horse's front leg upraised if the hero had been wounded in battle, and both front legs upraised if he had been killed on the battlefield. This statue neither stands nor sits. It walks, as pilgrims do. This is—or was, he corrected himself—a sculptor's rendition of Gandhi's most famous walk.

In 1930 he had walked from his ashram at Sabarmati to the seashore village of Dandi. He was sixty years old. It had taken him twenty-four days, stopping at villages along his way, to walk the two hundred and forty miles. He was walking to the coast to make salt from sea water in defiance of the British government's Salt Law that made Indian ownership of India's salt a criminal offence, and the Salt Tax an added burden on the poor.

Prabhakar had told his students the Salt March had been a unique event in politics. Gandhi had made no call for others to join him in breaking the Salt Law, but a trickle of followers had become thousands who joined the march at stages along the route. Across the country men and women made salt where they could. An Englishwoman walked with Gandhi. An Englishman wrote and people sang:

With dear old Gandhi, we'll all march
to Dandi,
And break all the salt laws that a white man
ever made.

Prabhakar had told his students this act of civil disobedience had become an ecstasy of civil disobedience. The power of civil disobedience had stirred people across nations and nationalities, and across the years. Thirty-five years after 1930, Martin Luther King and six hundred others had walked fifty-four miles from Selma to Montgomery in Alabama in their refusal to bow down to racial segregation. A month later two thousand more men and women, black and white, had marched again to Montgomery, walking all day and sleeping in the fields at night. There are ties stronger than blood, Prabhakar had told his class. There are ties beyond blood, beyond borders, beyond race and religion. Beyond.

'And this is why you stopped at the statue?' Sergei prompted.

'No, this is not why,' said Prabhakar.

He had stopped and parked across the road because of the demolition squad at work on it. They broke the legs first so that it would never walk again. This made the stone body fall forward for easy battering and breaking—as that other demolition squad Katerina had described, had done on women's bodies, disabling their legs first. He stayed to watch a machine pound the fallen body and lift the crushed stone to the storage space on top of the machine. He stayed watching the destruction to the end because it was a statue he would never see again. He stayed to say farewell to a unique political event and a page of Indian history—and as history has its human side, he stayed because Rahman's grandfather had been among the thousands who had walked with Gandhi on the Salt March.

Prabhakar felt a prickling like tears at the corners of his eyes and willed them not to fall.

'What about the procession of statues behind Gandhi?' asked Katerina, 'the people who followed him on the march? Did those statues get bulldozed too?'

'Those are still there, I suppose because they'll be following the statue they're planning to put up in Gandhi's place.'

'Anyone for Slivovitz?' Francois was beside them, gaily waving a bottle of plum brandy and calling for liqueur glasses. He poured it for them, said Salut, and Zdorovye to Sergei, and took the Slivovitz away.

'Something that happened a few days ago was much the same,' said Prabhakar, getting back to what had to be said, 'so demolition must be official policy now.'

He had gone with Rahman to the cemetery where Rahman's father and grandfather were buried, which his friend visited on their death anniversaries. On that immaculately kept kabristan, earth was being overturned by a giant excavator, digging up graves. Earth was flying and fragments falling in showers of bones and other human remains. An ancient tree had been felled and split open, obscenely exposing a century-old welter of ancient knotted roots. The guardian of the graveyard who had come from Moradabad as a young grave digger and grown old as its caretaker, sat at their feet, bowed over his knees, unable to watch this desecration of the last sacred resting place of the departed. The land was a jungle when I came, he wept, we made a garden of it for those who had left us. Sometimes we found bones while digging a new grave. Reverently, we would collect them, and place them prayerfully in the new grave we were digging.

To Rahman's question he had no answer or none he could bring himself to utter. The excavator's driver only knew he had orders but he told Rahman what he had heard: Burial is against our religion, we do not bury our dead, grounds that have been captured for burial will be dug up and prepared for national use. Rahman raised the old caretaker to his feet—they had on occasion stood side by side offering namaz in the mosque near the cemetery—and pressed the few hundred-rupee notes he was carrying into his hand. He'll be out of a job now, Rahman told Prabhakar, and homeless. He had been given quarters nearby for himself and his family and had lived there all these years.

Prabhakar clasped his friend's hand and stood holding it in shock and shared grief.

Sergei broke the solemn silence that followed Prabhakar's recital, saying, 'In Europe we think of wars about religion as belonging to the Middle Ages.'

'Here we are back to the Crusades,' said

Prabhakar, 'Our Popes have declared war on Islam.'

Sounds of happy leave-taking were coming from the hall. Thank-yous, long-drawn-out goodbyes, invisible hugs and kisses. Sergei thanked Prabhakar for giving him much to think about. Turning to Katerina he told her in Russian he had no words to express his sorrow for what she had been through.

'Not only me, Sergei. It's the treatment, and not just here. You must have read about the civil war in Yugoslavia in the 1990s, the one that eventually broke up the country.'

He must have, at the time, but it had made no special impression—one more Balkan disaster—and had soon become yesterday's news.

'Thousands of Muslim women—Bosnian, Croatian and Albanian—were rounded up and kept in camps to be raped by Christian Serbs. Those camps got known as rape camps. It's what war does to women but this was something new. Religious rape. Like here.'

It sounded fantastic in the extreme, a situation conjured up by a diseased and deranged imagination.

He had a passing doubt about the size and scale of it. So openly organized, would it not have made news outside its own terrain?

'One knows what war does, Katya,' he said slowly, 'Who doesn't? But I had never thought of it in terms of what happens to women.'

'No,' said Katerina, 'No one does.'

He acknowledged that yawning blank in the reckoning of war's damages. It reminded him of scorched earth laid waste and infertile by retreating armies.

After Sergei had gone, she bestirred herself and picked up her small silk purse. 'I must go. It's late.'

Prabhakar's mind had never been clearer than at this late hour of the night, and never so intent on making itself clear.

'Yes, it's time to go,' he agreed, 'but first there's something I want to say. You may be right that the tale has to be remembered and made known. Remember it and make it known if you must. But there's a life beyond that tale, a full and normal life.' He added, half-humorously, 'There's even a belief among us that there are lives beyond death.'

He looked hard at her, holding her gaze, 'So Katya, Katerina, however you wish to be called, there is life beyond gang rape. That's all I have to say except that I love you.'

Katerina pushed back her chair and stood up. 'Beyond must be your favourite word,' she said.

Unbelievably, she held out her hand. He took it with care, held it lightly, not imprisoning it with his other hand, and let it go. When the time came he would have to be as delicate with all the surfaces of her beautiful body in his awesome task of freeing her from her terror of being touched.

At his hotel Sergei phoned his daughter.

'Have you thought of a name, Daddy? Mum says you will want to keep names Russian in the family. '

'Your mother is right, Irina. We'll name the baby Katerina and she can be Katie for short. How is she doing?'

'Simply splendidly. Tom and I took her on an anti-war demonstration yesterday. That way it was easy for me to feed her when she was hungry and we could take turns carrying her in the sling. What? Oh, the sling is like a pouch you hang on your front.

It's a pouch to put the baby in. We put Katerina in it and she was snug and secure held against me—or Tom when he took over.'

'Irina, how old is she now?' Sergei tried to keep his agitation out of his voice. He knew better than to argue with Irina.

'She's nearly two months old.'

'And which war were you demonstrating against?'

'All war, of course. At last there's a politician who believes in unilateral disarmament like Tony Benn did. If he forms a party we're going to support him.'

Sergei tried, for his newborn granddaughter's sake, for fear of her being carried into the dust and uproar of future demonstrations slung in a sling, and for the sake of his own peace of mind to say cautiously, 'Well, there's no war on right now so there's no immediate need for action.'

Irina said wearily, as if she had said it time and again on public platforms—which she might well have done—yet with a consuming unfaltering passion, 'Do you realize, Daddy, that somewhere, in some part of the world, people are living in dread, scanning the sky for bombs? Somewhere else people are running for their lives in a city that's being devastated? We've heard Never Again so often, it's a joke. Daddy, there is nothing so certain as the certainty of the eternity of war. So someone has to say Stop.'

Sergei was well trained in her beliefs. Her single-mindedness always disturbed him afresh. What it was up against in a violent world was most disturbing of all. He tried to keep a recurring vision of physical harm to her out of his mind. Purity of heart was no protection against weapons of war. He was consoled by the thought that she and Tom had moved at his suggestion to the spacious upper floor of his apartment—once Susan's studio—after the baby's birth. To his relief they had agreed to give up their own two-room flat 'until we find something bigger we can afford. And it makes sense, Daddy, with all that space lying empty since Mum left and you away so much.'

He bid her a gentle goodnight and said he would be seeing her and Katerina very soon. He made no move to go to the bedroom and prepare for bed himself. The talk over dinner crowded out any notion of sleep. Finally, Dimitri's voice: No concern of ours. But Dimitri had not heard what he had heard tonight.

In the morning a late breakfast at Bonjour helped to restore his steady reliable perspective of affairs and he could look forward to the prospect of a morning's sightseeing. He ordered an unpronounceable, subtly flavoured Indian breakfast dish and ate it with new-found pleasure. The coffee surpassed itself. He glanced around the room. These particular paintings and tapestries which Francois and Prahlad had chosen with knowledge and care, and hung just this harmonious distance apart, in an atmosphere they had ensured would be unsullied by the vulgarity of competing loudness, had made for a space of order and beauty within four walls. Peace on earth in miniature. Wise men know this is what is meant by peace on earth and that we cannot change the world.

The telephone rang that night on his return from dinner with his company's agent.

'Sergei? It's me, Susan.'

He panicked. 'Is the baby all right? Irina?'

'I'm sorry I startled you, Sergei. Everyone's all right. I'm ringing to put your mind at rest. Irina told me you sounded worried when you talked to her.'

'I was frantic. I didn't know it showed.'

'Well, I'm ringing to say I've persuaded her to leave Katerina with me when she has to go to her meetings and demonstrations and she's agreed.'

His relief was profound. Only Susan could have persuaded her. Susan had always been a confident mother, well able to take care of their two children during his frequent absences and it was obvious she had lost none of her sure and sensitive touch, based on their mutual respect for one another's opinions. Their two children, but for Susan, might have gone their separate ideological ways without a care for each other, Sergei acknowledged in silent gratitude. He asked if she would come to dinner the day after he got back so that they could have a family evening together. Susan was doubtful. She was having dinner with Philip and his new author to show them the rather unusual cover she had designed for the novel Philip was publishing, but she would try and change the date. Since Sergei had first met her and wooed her, her politics had been confined to the book covers she designed. A cover she had designed for a biography of Hitler had shown him a tiny figure in the lower right-hand corner, with Wehrmacht marchers glitteringly occupying the main cover front and back.

Prabhakar pushed aside the papers he was correcting to answer the telephone. It was Lisette. She was buoyant. She had glorious news. She was getting married next month to the owner of the set-up for whom she had investigated Indian food and they were going to open a restaurant. It would be the only one of its kind in London or anywhere in England. It would be purely Mughal, with décor to match.

'We want Rafeeq to come here. With his family, of course, if he has one. We'll make all the arrangements as soon as he agrees. Could you talk to him and let me know?'

Normally Prabhakar would have asked her how this would be possible with the immigration hurdles now being put in place, and impossible at any time for people like Rafeeq, but the bare fact was 'He's not at the kaif any more.'

'Why ever not? Where is he?'

Prabhakar cast about for a way to explain that would not sound like gibberish, but there was no rational explanation. 'Rafeeq is not at the kaif because it's not safe to cook mutton any more in case the Cow Commission says it's beef.'

'You're joking, Prabhu,' she said, incredulous, 'And then what?'

'Then you're arrested, or worse. You could be killed.'

'What's happening?' she demanded, 'I don't understand.'

Prabhakar had seldom been at a loss for words but what words were there to describe what had never happened before. Never here. A new gross jargon would have to be learned. As Lisette was struck dumb he continued, 'So there's no Mughal cooking at the kaif any more. There's no Mughal anything any more, not even the empire. They've taken it out of history books.'

Lisette recovered to say vigorously, 'But that's

absolute nonsense. It's as daft as saying we never had the Tudors, all the Henrys and Elizabeth One. It sounds as ridiculous as a nursery rhyme I learned when I was six years old:

Hey diddle diddle, the cat and the fiddle, the cow jumped over the moon,
The little dog laughed to see such fun and the dish ran away with the spoon.'

'That explains our situation perfectly,' said Prabhakar.

'Well, I don't understand what it's all about,' she said, getting back to the purpose of her call, 'but we have to have Rafeeq for our new restaurant. He's authentic, a real find. No one else will do. Look Prabhu, I know he'll be nervous about coming here. It's a big step for him to take. But you must persuade him, and tell him he won't regret it. We'll take good care of him and if he has children we'll put them in school…'

'Lisette, Rafeeq is not at his home. There's no one there. If I can find him I'll let you know.' How he would find Rafeeq he had no idea, but the effort would have to be made. Lisette was a person who saw things through. 'And congratulations. Your news is wonderful.'

'I'm in heaven, Prabhu. But we must have Rafeeq.'

A suggestion came from Katerina at dinner that night at Rahman's. 'Rafeeq's home must be in one of the areas they're driving people out of and setting fire to, like the village I was assigned and other villages around there, or digging up grounds like the graveyard. They call it taking back the land occupied by invaders.'

Rahman had been unlike himself, unnaturally subdued since the excavation of the graveyard. It was Salma who asked where the villagers driven out of their homes had gone. Katerina didn't know, but one of her colleagues and co-writer on their book project had said that in her country the policy of wiping out a religion had herded whole families into camps, made displaced people of them while it was decided what to do next. These were very primitive makeshift shelters with no proper sanitation or water supply or electricity. People had to rig up their own electric wiring and scrounge around for wood to cook on.

'How did she know? Did she see one of these camps?' asked Salma.

'She lived in one of them. She was one of the herd driven into them. She said guards used to come at night and separate the women from the men...'

Katerina sensed violent recoil like a live presence in the room and gave it a minute before continuing, 'We will have to find out where those villagers are, if they've been put in a camp, and go there. ' Another second of silence told her no one else's mind had jumped ahead to that course of action. 'Of course, Rafeeq may not be there but that's where he's most likely to be. We'll have to go and see.'

She must not go with them, they protested. Rahman, with his habitual tenderness for mankind and more especially for womankind, said it would be exhausting and emotionally too much of a strain after all she had been through. As if she hadn't heard, Katerina told them she would make enquiries tomorrow morning and go with them. She had never met Rafeeq and wouldn't recognize him, but Rahman had said he had a wife and two children so she would ask among the women. It could be useful. It had to be agreed she would go with them tomorrow afternoon after classes, giving her the morning to find out where the camp, if there was one, was located.

At the sprawl of tents, hutments and flimsier shelters concocted out of tin and tarpaulin, Katerina suggested they divide up for a thorough search for Rafeeq, not just look around for him but keep asking if anyone knew him or had seen him. Prabhakar took the direction given. He had not imagined quite this. There was a finality about this mass removal, clearly no hope of escape from it. There would be no going back to where they had come from, or forward to elsewhere, for those expelled from their village lands and their livelihoods who now had nothing to do and nowhere to go. This squalor had no shape or form and no connection with anything he thought of as human habitation. Yet human voices were telling him they knew no one called Rafeeq; the sun was beating down on barefoot children chasing each other through the mud of narrow alleys between shelters or playing marbles in the dirt; an infant howling behind a makeshift curtain of cloth thrown over a rope, was soothed, lulled, and must have slept; cooking fires were being fanned, hot sparks flying into the hot air. He walked on through the sound of men's voices, the chatter of quarrelling children, a woman pounding clothes in the scanty water from a tap—signs of humanity obstinately alive in the nowhere of displacement. In a patch of shade two old men squatted, staring into space. They, at least, had recognized the permanence of their plight. Coming to a tent at the end of his area he called out and lifted a tent flap by its corner, hoping to get some information from those within, and let it drop, paralysed by his transgression. A woman labouring strenuously to give birth lay on straw matting on the ground, her legs wide open, her body writhing, her groans unmindful of all but the merciless rhythm of labour. The woman keeping vigil between her legs had paid him no attention.

He walked back, his stomach convulsed by the sight and sounds of birthing, the ultimate act in defiance of extermination.

On their way home, an hour's drive, Rahman at the wheel, there was little to be said about the failure of their mission. Their separate silences bound them closer than talk. Prabhakar, sitting beside Rahman, felt sickened at the thought that Rafeeq might have been beaten to death and his body left rotting on some roadside. Where could his family be hiding and how long could they hide? He understood why Rahman had nothing to say. In deep mourning for the man he had known, for the faith they had shared, and for their brotherhood with all others under the Indian sun, what is there to say? Prabhakar turned to see if Katerina was all right, more out of his need to look at her, an opportunity that rarely came his way. Her head was leaning against the seat back, her eyes were closed, her mouth slightly open. Her hands had fallen far apart as if unrelated to each other. One must have slipped off her lap and lay looking lifeless beside her on the seat, the other looking as lifeless on the other far side of her lap. Sweat had left her hair limp and lank on her shoulders and dried on her face, leaving a damp sheen of it on her forehead. Sleep had released her to an abandonment that the discipline of her waking hours did not allow. He had never seen her more desirable or loved her more passionately than in this unconscious disarray. As they got back to town their jerky progress through traffic woke her and she directed Rahman to her house. There was a semblance of a return to ordinariness in her instructions to drive straight on, turn right at the next crossing, it's the last house in the lane. At the porch overhung by its curtain of bougainvillea, she said, 'Come in and wash and have a cold drink.' Automatically they obeyed. Cooled and freshened by soap and water, sipping their ice-filled glasses of lemon juice, they were somewhat revived but not yet recovered from what they had seen, and fearful of what might have happened to Rafeeq. They thanked Katerina for coming with them on their expedition and being of the greatest help.

Katerina shook her head, frowning. She dismissed their thanks. What were they talking about? Of course she had had to go to see the camp. It was vital to keep track of what was going on. Hadn't they realized there may be other camps, considering the new policy? Her voluntary group might decide to do an investigation into these. She added as a matter of interest, 'One thinks one's own is the ultimate catastrophe, and of course it is, but only for oneself.'

'An investigation?' echoed Rahman in disbelief, 'Like your last one? Would that be wise?'

Katerina was astonished that he should ask such a question. 'No,' she replied, 'Of course it wouldn't,' and saw them out to Rahman's car.

American voices filled the room that was full of Indians. Trays were offering American cocktails among other drinks.

'I've heard so much about you, we all have. What a pleasure to meet you. Mr Mirajkar has told us about your book and your presentation at his get-together.'

The woman's voice had no cocktail party bubble about it. The woman herself, in solid middle age, looked like a person in authority. Prabhakar could see her chairing a meeting with professional ease, with an American insistence on the facts, figures and data which established proof. Americans were known to deal in ground realities, not fairy tales. They had Hollywood for those.

He had made up his mind to refuse this invitation to a reception for visiting dignitaries at the Century Hotel. Obviously, Mirajkar had put him on the guest list and he wanted to end his uncomfortable association with the Master Mind, but Rahman had advised, 'Better go. Get the atmospherics. As Katerina said, it's just as well to know what's going on.'

'Let me introduce myself,' she said, giving her name and the name of the company she worked for, 'I'm one of the VHA. We're the Voice of Hindu Americans—which makes us your voice in the United States—and I'm happy to say we're getting a lot of support from the administration. I know how worried people here are about the new immigration policy—though in all fairness one can hardly blame the USA for clamping down on immigration, everyone is doing it—but my Senator is working on trying to get Hindus into the white category so our people here won't have to go through all the usual hoops when they apply for visas, or for citizenship.'

White category? She clarified this meant that though Hindus would not be in the privileged category of the European Union whose members needed no visas, they would be upgraded for entry to the USA, or for citizenship. 'If my Senator gets his proposal through it would make Hindu Indians honorary whites... but I'm keeping you from helping yourself to a drink, here comes a bearer.'

The only drinks left on the passing tray were dry martinis and he took one. Recklessly. There was always a first time. He took a swallow of it and hated its harshness.

He knew he was being annoyingly slow to appreciate and applaud the VHA's role in this forthcoming achievement. 'But how can Indians be put into the white category?' he asked.

'Not all Indians,' she corrected, 'we've too much

of a muddle of races, which, of course, is being put right now, but no, no, this will only apply to Hindus, not those who came as invaders and other outsiders. We are the only ones who have a right to the white category. You know, Mr Prabhakar, there's an enormous amount of sympathy for what Hindus are going through here. But in any case there is such a thing as a racial hierarchy and we belong at the top, to the Indo-European racial category. It's been the VHA's job to acquaint the administration in the United States with this fact and we circulate it in the media and women's clubs and other influential groups. We're covering a lot of ground and we've had a generally favourable response. After all, it takes no great leap of imagination to understand a historical fact, and it's as much an anthropological fact. A well-known historian has vouched for it, as you may have read.'

Alerted by the martini Prabhakar noticed a map behind the cocktail bar at his end of the room. The cartographer had fancied an India extending from the Indus in the far north to the Arabian Sea at its southern tip as one unbroken landscape of lustrous gold. No obstruction had been permitted to mar the peninsula between the snows and the sea, no Afghanistan, no Pakistan, no Bangladesh. For the country he had invented, the cartographer-turned-artist had invented a colour, this pale lustrous gold never seen before on any map of any country. Prabhakar's informant followed his glance and nodded as if in complete approval of his dumb amazement.

'Makes one catch one's breath, doesn't it? Let's just say it's an artistic vision of the future.'

She greeted someone across the room and took her smiling leave. Prabhakar described the map to Rahman afterwards, saying it was not a figment of his imagination, and nor was the martini responsible for what he saw.

'It seemed to sum up the occasion,' he said.

'It sums up everything,' retorted Rahman.

The Sunday paper always had a lavishly illustrated supplement. Pictures of classical singers and dancers, film-makers, writers and other creative achievers—the truly great—as well as food and fashion, were splashed over its pages. But the American ambassador was featured under a headline on the front page of the main newspaper. Prabhakar read: 'The Ambassador of the United States, His Excellency Mr Jake Judson and his wife, are seen at the foot of the aircraft. In his farewell message Mr Judson said he had high hopes of India. It had been a privilege to serve here at a time when major changes are taking place and more are expected. He complimented the government for the reforms it had undertaken, and affirmed the alliance between "our two great democracies."'

There were times when Prabhakar, who was not a Communist, wished he was. This was one of them. He hoped Communism had a future. He turned the page. Nothing much there of interest. He glanced down the page and an item in small print caught his eye. Vandals had broken into a restaurant called Bonjour. The damage was yet to be assessed...

Prabhakar got no reply from either Prahlad's or Francois's numbers. He dressed hurriedly and drove to Bonjour. The cluster of flowerpots at the entrance to the stairway had been smashed, the hydrangeas and other blooms flattened under a heavy muddy tread. He went upstairs. The glass door to the restaurant was open minus its glass. He walked through its empty wooden frame. Prahlad was standing in a sea of shattered glass, facing a bare wall. The French paintings of springtime flowers that had hung on the wall lay knifed to shreds around his feet. The Tree of Life opposite had been pulled off its wall, scissored and trampled. Chairs had been overturned. Some lay broken. A table had lost its legs. Prahlad was in a state of shock. Prabhakar went up to him, took his arm and turned him around to lead him to an unbroken chair. Two men came in. One of them pushed Prabhakar aside. Prabhakar resisted instinctively, enraged. The intruder's arm swung out and hit him in the face. Prabhakar staggered backwards and fell. Blood smeared his face. He tasted it in his mouth. On his feet again rage drove him to retaliate. He was wrenched back by the other intruder who followed instructions to 'deal with him so that we can get on with our business.'

Prabhakar was dealt with. He was left on the floor gagged and bound with rope. 'Prahlad, is it?' he heard their wheedling voices, 'then why no divine protection if you are Prahlad?' Prabhakar heard and smelled a match being struck, blearily saw it held to the soles of Prahlad's feet and heard Prahlad's long-drawn-out howl of unbearable pain. And then once more. 'So, Prahlad you cannot be. Fire did not burn Prahlad. What are you?' One of the wheedlers enquired of the other, 'Do his kind at least have balls the same as us?' They pulled his pants down and dealt with what they saw. 'They're no use to the likes of him.' Prabhakar heard screams faded out by their laughter and then, 'Enough. The order was to smash the place and fix the dancer. No more holy dances for the likes of him.' He heard their heavy tread thudding down the stairs. A lifetime later he felt a movement ungagging him. Francois's voice said he had been at the police station, held up there like an offender and questioned for an hour. Prabhakar's rope was untied. He was helped to his knees and eventually to his feet. Rocking on his feet he helped Francois to untruss Prahlad. Between them they got his trousers on. He could not be stood up on his tortured feet. He had to be lifted down the stairs with help from Bonjour's cook who had stayed hidden in the kitchen. The day wore on as Prabhakar got himself down the stairs.

At the hospital Francois stayed with Prahlad. Prabhakar was examined by an elderly doctor who said it must have been a terrible accident. Thrown out, you say? Hit by a speeding truck? There were all too many such accidents these days.

Lies have to be told when the truth is too dangerous.

The abdominal injuries are severe and will take time to heal. An ice pack for your eye and your face. These medicines and it goes without saying a few days' rest in bed. But all things considered…The doctor, a kindly man with an old-fashioned regard for a patient's fears smiled reassuringly, conveying good, if not the best, news.

Prabhakar rang Rahman who came after his class and helped him into his car.

'What did the doctor say?' asked Rahman, 'No, don't talk if it hurts. I saw Francois. Couldn't see

Prahlad. He's in a bad way. How could this have happened?' he wondered, 'The Master Mind? His policymakers, considering their anti-nature, anti-religion, anti-our-culture tirades against gays?'

'And the Mood,' mumbled Prabhakar, 'Europe. Here. Everywhere. Hate. Kill.'

'Your fault, dost, you wrote a book, remember? Like Mary Shelley you let loose a monster.' A feeble attempt at a joke, but one that brought an effort at a crooked smile to his friend's swollen face. Rahman put an arm around him in a half-embrace.

At Prabhakar's apartment he helped him into bed, said he and Salma would come round in the evening, and left.

Bed rest allowed him the leisure to go over it all, but not the luxury of forgetting. The body had a memory of its own. On his third day of rest, the bell rang though he had requested friends not to come. This one called, 'Where are you?' and putting the ice pack aside he directed Katerina to his bedroom. She stood beside his bed. Looking down and right through his body on the bed, she said she had been to see Prahlad. Parts of him were better but he would never dance again. And you? Of habit he took in the startling beauty of her, unbelievably physically present in his room. He was all right, he said, just resting as ordered. Lies that had to be told.

'So I see,' she said, 'I've been away, I just got back so I just heard about it from Francois. I was in Leningrad with my mother, visiting my grandmother.'

There was something odd about that sentence of hers. What was it? Yes, Leningrad. It had not been called Leningrad for years. She should have called it Petrograd or St Petersburg, he'd forgotten what name it went by. Was she looking forward to a Communist future? His political mind told him that when there is one extreme, as there is here, you have to swing all the way to the other extreme before coming back to an ideal space in the middle. The feminists had understood that. During his lack of response Katerina had not sat down on the chair near his bed. Any moment she would be gone and he would be left with the times he had made love to her in his imagination, with a delicate care for her recoil from touch. Instead, a modern miracle. She lay down beside him and eased one arm around and under him. He felt it under his shoulder blades, supporting his back. Her free hand rested on his abdomen before tracing the path lovemaking took in a reversal of their roles, bringing his body, the corpse it had been, to ardent life. The holy books were not wrong.

Susan had been able to change her date with her publisher and came to dinner the day after Sergei returned. She had also rung Ivan and told him he must fly over for a day or two and meet his new niece—now asleep in her carrycot on the living room floor—and spend a little time with all of them. Dinner, ordered by Susan, had been a comfortable return to familiar home-cooked food after exotic menus abroad. Sergei had the weekend ahead for a long slow unwinding. He sat back listening to Tom and Ivan arguing. It was the kind of academic argument they had on the subject from time to time, by now without raising their voices, to reaffirm their known positions. As always it was well informed on both sides, with neither side (in Sergei's opinion) getting the better of the other, the subject being what it was and both of them being right.

Tonight Tom was asking Ivan what new weapon of destruction was on the anvil. In Tom's opinion, bombs and missiles and all that cumbersome heavyweight war-making stuff would be as out of date as bows and arrows very soon with all the new research into deadly chemicals that would make napalm look as harmless as lavender water. No armies and no armaments would be needed. Poisoning the air or making a drought would do the needful. Wouldn't that put the family firm out of business? Ivan said it would make no difference at all. He didn't believe weapons of any kind would be going out of date. Dimitri's grandson speaking, observed Sergei, with a loyalty to the family firm and a business-like commitment to its product that would have rejoiced Dimitri. He would have known the firm was safe in Ivan's capable hands. Sergei had never been able to summon the wholeheartedness that would have rewarded his father's efforts to build a future from scratch. All that Sergei had done in return was to put away his ifs and buts and follow his father, as a filial duty, into the business, working hard and commendably but with a secret sense of betrayal of the life he would otherwise have made for himself. Even then it had not been a matter of conscience but of the classics he would have preferred to indulge in, and an urge to write.

'The weapons you use,' he heard Ivan explain, 'depend on what kind of war you're planning to make—sky, ground, or chemical, or all three. And that decision depends on what you are aiming to destroy and what you have to be careful not to: the sites of copper or diamonds or oil or uranium or whatever your war is going to be about.'

From Tom: 'It also seems to depend on which country you're planning to attack and what colour the people are who live there. The atom bomb wasn't invented for Europe and all the baby atom bombs they've been dropping since then have been on Africa.'

'Well, there you have it, Tom. End of argument.'

Irina said, 'It's not the end of what's going on.

Did you know that in Nigeria Africans are fighting foreign oil companies for control of their own oil? What right do companies have to grab someone else's oil or uranium or other resources?'

'It's not about rights, Irina. It's about trade and being in control of it. It's what empires were about. Trade is what makes the world go round. You have to keep the upper hand. You don't need to occupy Asia and Africa to do that any more. You just stay in control by making sure your kind of people are in power over there.'

Irina countered, 'And knowing your guns could be bumping off an elected leader like Lumumba and so many others, you can still…?' Irina gave up mid-sentence.

Sergei drank his coffee, recalling that in his youth after-dinner conversation had been about books and plays, or the latest political scandal. Tom and Ivan would go on arguing, but there was no final answer—given the permanence of war—to the rights or wrongs of catering for it, which was the job of the armaments trade and a simple matter of demand and supply. The argument, as Sergei well knew, had no end. It had gone around in his own head since he entered the business his father had so painstakingly built. The two opposite views held by his children had kept it simmering, and the dinner talk at Francois's had given it a new lease of life. The sight of a war victim—which Katerina was— had made sure that for him the argument would not obligingly go away. Her wounds were glaring evidence of war and there was written evidence otherwise of the event she had unemotionally laid before him. But he had had a flicker of doubt about the camps she had spoken of, set up when civil war was tearing Yugoslavia apart. Large numbers obscure reality. Pain, one's own or another's, is hard to quantify, and memory can make mistakes. But he had looked up the period to establish the facts and found that Katerina had not exaggerated. The rape camps had been as real as the gas chambers. Women, as she had pointed out, had always been war booty, to be carted away with other loot by the winner. But this, she had said, was not that time-worn routine, it was different, and Sergei's information had left him in no doubt that the concentration camps for mass rape had been officially ordered, efficiently organized, and had served their purpose, it seemed, with spectacular success. Hard evidence had been provided by the international tribunal appointed by the court at The Hague to investigate the facts. It was obvious the camps were carrying out political policy of the gas chamber variety, as monstrous as that final solution had been, to isolate, despoil, and demolish large numbers of the unwanted. The court at The Hague had branded it a war crime.

There is no accounting for the particular moment that says enough is enough and there is no drama about the decision then taken. The responsibility for running an industry that depended on wars and catered for them had come to an end for Sergei when he verified the facts. He felt curiously light, unburdened and uninvolved as he listened to Ivan talk of supply and demand being the nature of the arms trade, and heard Tom replying that this could be said of a brothel. The argument ended in a draw, the young people discussed plans for the weekend and dispersed to their rooms. Sergei took Susan to the apartment he had bought for her, saw her safely in—old habits die hard—and said let's meet soon. He came home to think about what he would do in retirement, but one step at a time. His first step would be the book waiting these many years to be written.

He sketched out a rough approach at his desk over the weekend. Conquest, occupation, and control of the seized land's treasures were a long-established progression. Nothing new there. But never had seizure of lands and treasure been envisaged as a birthright until Cecil Rhodes. And never had politics, industry, and armaments worked in such harmony to achieve the desired result. In truth, there had been a symphonic harmony about the entire process with Rhodes as its conceiver, composer and conductor. What his country owed him had made a national hero of him. There were statues of him and a film celebrating 'Rhodes of Africa'. Hero-worship had inspired the 1892 cartoon in *Punch* of Rhodes, legs spread wide, straddling the length of Africa from Cairo to the Cape, his arms flung east and west, his body slung with an assault rifle that showed how possession had been accomplished.

The cartoon paid homage to a nineteenth-century Caesar, a colossus whose promise of 'Tomorrow the world' predated Hitler by decades. Rhodes' belief in his right to own Africa—'those parts that are at present inhabited by the most despicable specimens of human beings'—had come from his belief in imperial destiny, a phrase he himself might have concocted, and maybe he had, so smoothly did it serve his philosophy. Over port and cigars with policymakers and the moneymen of industry and armaments, he had laid down the doctrine of divine right. The white race being the master race, so ably represented by the English upper class, the British empire had a divine right to conquer and rule the 'uncivilized world'. He had shown how this could be done by doing it, combining in himself all three ingredients for control: He had become prime minister of Cape Colony and made himself de facto ruler of vast lands in southern Africa; he had spent extravagantly on armaments to clear those tribal lands of their inhabitants, for gold and diamond mining—'I prefer land to niggers'—and he had become a diamond billionaire.

All this was old hackneyed imperial sin, mused Sergei, leafing through his Rhodes material. The sentiments, the language, the 'destiny' that sanitized brutality were familiar features of long-gone imperial times and imperial crimes. What reading Rhodes made clear, however, was that a version of divine right still ruled the planet and the formula for the capture and control of commerce still relied heavily, if not always openly, on arms. A rose by any other name, or devil in disguise, depending on your angle of vision. 'Devil in Disguise' sounded like an apt summary of a post-Rhodes post-imperial world still bolstered by the force of arms and might be an apt title for a book. It was a curious situation in this day and age, but that being the case, was he, Sergei, to infer that by merely doing his job, as he had done, or by obeying orders as Nuremburg's accused Nazis had done, one missed the fact of one's own involvement in crime? By this logic had he been accessory to the murder of unknown millions?

It was after midnight when this vaguely disquieting night-time thought struck him. It was the sort of abstraction he had no use for, too vague, too theatrical. But daylight altered it hardly at all in his favour when by chance he came across a document he had not seen since his return, left among his papers by Irina probably, as she sometimes did to bring words worth remembering to his notice. This time it was a speech against the Cold War and all war. He read it with growing surprise. These were not, as he would have expected, the routine sentiments of a pacifist or anarchist or some woolly-headed idealist spouting the usual spiel. These were the words of a five-star general of the American army who had become president of the United States, in a formal speech delivered at the White House. Sergei read President Eisenhower's grim warning against the 'military–industrial complex', branding it a formidable threat to democracy, and, as his words suggested, to a just and humane society: 'Every gun that is made, every warship launched, every rocket fired, signifies, in the final sense, a theft from those who hunger and are not fed, those who are cold and are not clothed. This world in arms is not spending money alone. It is spending the sweat of its labourers, the genius of its scientists, the hopes of its children…Under the cloud of threatening war, it is humanity hanging from a cross of iron.'

During the days that followed, Sergei's approach to the book he was going to write took a direction of its own, one he had certainly not intended. His own rough idea had been to narrate the fascinating story of trade in readable language for the general reader: from its quaint and colourful beginnings to international importance. But now that would be the first half of the story. The second half would go from baubles and beads to bombs; from footsore plodding to soaring threatening power; from Dimitri's escape for survival and the second life that made a fortune on arms supplied to specific wars. There was no shortage of material, preserved in the company's archives, of the figures made on armaments deals during the Cold War—he recalled Dimitri's example of the Communist bloodbath in Indonesia—and finally, the peacetime deals that had funded peacetime wars in his own time. What would this be, a much delayed reckoning? A confession to assuage guilt for crimes committed? A bid for absolution, as in the confessional? Sergei did not have a melodramatic turn of mind. He had no idea how the story would develop as he wrote it, only that in the light of Eisenhower's unheeded warning, the warning needed to be revived.

Not much came by post these days but this handsome square of vellum could have come no other way. Prabhakar drew out the card embossed with fine gold lettering. It was an invitation to Lisette's wedding. To nobility, it appeared. She had not told him the food entrepreneur she was going to marry was in the titled, privileged, nearly royal class, Lisette whom he had had the audacity to take through sweltering heat and meandering cows and buffalos to the kaif. But knowing himself he would have done so even had he known her background and lofty connections. And knowing Lisette, she had not mentioned, or had simply forgotten to, that her intended was kin to royalty because it had not occurred to her that this information was of any importance compared with the rapture of being in love. It was going to be a church wedding, Lisette ecstatic in bridal white, trailing a diaphanous veil, making vows to a man who Prabhakar hoped would be worthy of this exceptional woman, one who could surprise you with some new aspect of herself every five minutes.

There was a letter enclosed. She wrote, 'You must come, Prabhu, and bring a companion. We shall pay your fare and your wedding stay. We won't take no for an answer. It will be our gratitude to you for introducing me to the kaif. But for that visit we would not be opening our fabulous new restaurant.' Prabhakar was happy for her that she had seen fit to go ahead with her cherished plan and knowing Lisette, she would have found, somewhere on earth or a nearby planet, exactly the chef of her choice. The next para said: 'Please look at the gorgeous invitation to the opening of The Mughal which I designed. I've sent it to you by email. That's where we'll be having our wedding lunch party.'

Prabhakar did so and downloaded the invitation requesting the pleasure of his company. It was indeed special. Beautifully designed it was, as though on turquoise silk, and cunningly lettered to resemble Persian calligraphy. Lisette had attended to every detail with imagination and in her meticulous fashion. He scrolled further to the chef pictured on one side of the invitation—an unusual touch—elegantly attired in Mughal costume. Prabhakar was dumbfounded. He was looking at Rafeeq. This was Rafeeq elegantly attired, alive and well and prospering on Lisette's invitation. He enlarged the picture and there was no mistaking him.

He held his impatience and mounting irritation in check until late that evening when he rang Lisette.

'I know, I know, Prabhu, I do apologize but I couldn't tell you earlier. It was a question of secrecy, not knowing if he would be found and how to get him out if he was. Jimmy's uncle who's an absolute darling is the high commissioner in India and in all secrecy we appealed to him to consider the circumstances, explaining the danger Rafeeq was in after you told me what might happen to him. Jimmy's uncle was superb. He's dealt with these ghastly situations before and he has strong views. Don't ask me how they located Rafeeq but they did

The Fate of Butterflies

and kept him and his wife and two children on the official premises till their passports could be made and their passage arranged... Yes, I know, Prabhu, but as Rafeeq already had a job waiting for him here, and Jimmy's uncle had assured the authorities he was in the skilled category, there was no problem.'

The news was such a relief that Prabhakar found it hard to go on being angry with her for not telling him earlier and sparing him and Rahman their fears for Rafeeq's life and their own endless anxiety.

'Am I forgiven, Prabhu? Are we still friends? And you will come to the wedding and the opening, won't you?'

He said he had a better idea. A close friend of his, Rahman, who knew Rafeeq and his family much better than he did and had been in great distress about him, would be the perfect person to go, along with his wife. Lisette was disappointed but readily agreed.

'And there's another reason why I can't come, Lisette. I'm getting married too.'

Her small shriek of pure delight served as congratulation. But what about all the antecedents he didn't have? Prabhakar said Katerina had told him she had enough and to spare for both of them, including uncles and aunts. About to say more he condensed it for the hidden listener, saying the hey diddle diddle situation here needed his attention. Lisette was quick to understand. He put the phone down. Katerina sat across from him, waiting to resume their life together. The frightening mixture of joy and dread that the sight of her and the dangers of her work evoked, welled up in him. Love knows no safe haven in times like these. Yet Prahlad with his unerring instinct had given all lovers the only answer to that when he announced so jubilantly on that happiest of evenings: The times are grim, the times are unbearably tragic, and so, my friends— let's dance!